PUFFIN BOOKS

Editor: Kaye Webb

HERO TALES FROM THE BRITISH ISLES

All the world worships a hero, and every part of Britain has its own legends about men of glorious valour and derring-do.

In this collection you will find all the great names, from Cuchulain the champion warrior who single-handed defended Ulster against the whole army of Connaught, to Taliesin the Welsh boy who became a famous poet, prophet and magician.

There are plenty of rousing stories, but the romantic ones are the most haunting. Deirdre's lament for her slain brothers, and the legend that Arthur and his knights lie sleeping in a cave until Britain needs them, have a poetry which will last forever.

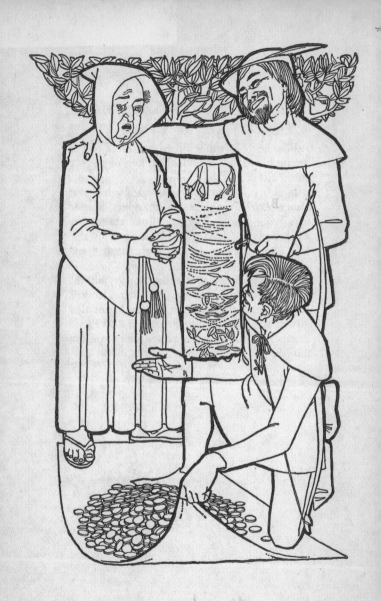

HERO TALES
FROM THE
BRITISH ISLES

retold by
BARBARA LEONIE PICARD

illustrations by
GAY GALSWORTHY

PUFFIN BOOKS

Puffin Books, Penguin Books Ltd, Harmondsworth, Middlesex, England
Penguin Books, 625 Madison Avenue, New York, New York, 10022, U.S.A.
Penguin Books Australia Ltd, Ringwood, Victoria, Australia
Penguin Books Canada Ltd, 41 Steelcase Road West, Markham, Ontario, Canada
Penguin Books (N.Z.) Ltd, 182–190 Wairau Road, Auckland 10, New Zealand

—

First published by Edmund Ward 1963
Published in Puffin Books 1966
Reprinted 1969, 1971, 1975, 1976

—

—

Made and printed in Great Britain
by Hazell Watson & Viney Ltd,
Aylesbury, Bucks
Set in Linotype Juliana

Contents

Preface

IN this book are retold the stories of a few of the folk heroes of the British Isles: legendary figures whose exploits have inspired or entertained the people of these islands for century after century. In the introductions and postscripts to the tales, I have tried to give a little of the history of these heroic figures: how they have their roots in Britain's most ancient past, and how they have changed down the years to become as they are known today. I have also tried to show, both by those legends chosen for inclusion, and in my notes, the manner in which many of the heroes link up with each other in one way or another, and how similarly they have evolved in the course of centuries. There is no need for anyone who does not care to do so to read these introductions and notes, as the stories are all complete in themselves, but I hope that those who read them will find that they bring an added interest to the tales.

At the end of the book is a short note on the pronunciation of certain of the names occurring in the stories, which may be of help to readers.

B.L.P.

ENGLAND

Arthur, King of Britain

Because of Sir Thomas Malory's magnificent retelling of so many of the Arthurian legends, we are apt to think of King Arthur and his men in fifteenth-century armour, as though they had been contemporaries of Malory. And then, unable to fit him into the fifteenth century of the history books, we tend to dismiss him as a mere fairy-tale hero who never really lived.

There was almost certainly a historical Arthur, a British chieftain and military leader who fought against the Saxon invaders, after the Romans had gone from Britain. Such a figure will undoubtedly have had a strong hold on popular imagination, and after his death exaggerated and fanciful stories of his exploits will have been told. Then, as so often with a folk-hero, he will have taken the place of the central character in far older tales, have acquired the attributes of more ancient heroes, the gods and demi-gods of days long past, and he will have been accompanied on his mythical adventures – either his own adventures or those which he usurped – by companions from an earlier legendary cycle. By the time we come to Malory's retellings, little remains either of the warrior chieftain of history or of the demi-god of mythology. But if we look below the surface of Malory's tales, beneath the elaborate fifteenth-century armour of his heroes, beyond the stilted courtesy of his own times, and behind the veneer of Christianity, we shall find traces of far older things which Malory and his contemporaries will not have dreamt lay hidden there.

Arthur and his knights are the subject of a number of English ballads and tales and of several Welsh legends, but the Welsh Arthur is a far more mysterious and evasive figure than the English Arthur, and therefore closer to the old British gods with whose exploits he has been credited. Malory collected the material for his Morte d'Arthur from many sources, including French Arthurian tradition. This accounts for the many inconsistencies and contradictions in the episodes which he relates.

Malory's Sir Kay the Seneschal is usually shown in the adventures in which he takes part as an ill-tempered bully, notable neither for his skill at arms nor for his courtesy. The Kei of Welsh legend, on the other hand, is a respected hero, second only to Arthur himself. In the episode of the five kings, however, the exploits of Malory's Kay would not be inappropriate to Kei.

The other great Arthurian hero who fares less well in Malory's pages than he does in the English ballads and in Welsh tradition, is Arthur's nephew, Sir Gawaine. As the great opponent in the Morte d'Arthur of Sir Lancelot – a latecomer to the Arthurian cycle from French romance – Gawaine is bound to receive less than his due, since Malory's sympathy is with Lancelot. Gawaine – the Welsh Gwalchmei, 'Hawk of May' – is, like Cuchulain of Ulster, a solar hero. Even in the Morte d'Arthur this is still plain, for Malory tells us that when fighting, Gawaine's strength increased every hour until midday, and then decreased hourly when noon was past. As Gawaine is light and virtue, so his brother Mordred – the Welsh Medrawt – is darkness and evil; and in this they correspond to the old British gods, Lleu Llaw Gyffes, the sun god, and his brother Dylan.

Malory's Sir Bedivere, who was with Arthur at the last, is

the Bedwyr of earlier Welsh tradition, whose name, together with that of Kei, is usually found at the head of any list of Arthur's bravest followers.

IN the very far-off days a king of Britain died, leaving three young sons, the eldest of whom was no more than a boy. A lord of Britain named Vortigern caused the new young king to be murdered and would have slain his two brothers, Aurelius and Uther, also, but that their mother fled with them from the land. Thereupon Vortigern made himself king of Britain.

Now, this was at a time when enemies of Britain would come over the sea in ships and try to seize the kingdom for themselves, and Vortigern wished to raise a mighty stronghold against them. He called together his men and set them to build a fortress on the top of a hill in Wales. They dug a wide ditch all about the hill, and brought stones from the countryside around that they might make a high wall within the ditch; but though they laboured on the wall all day, each night that portion of the wall which they had built would fall down of itself, untouched by the hand of any man. Vortigern sent for his wise men and asked them the reason for this, but of them all, only one made him any answer.

'The wall will stand, lord,' he said, 'only when the mortar which you use is mixed with the blood of a boy who has no father.'

Vortigern, trusting in the saying of this man, sent messengers over all the land; and though at first their quest seemed hopeless, at last they found by chance a nine-year-old boy of whom it was said that he had no earthly father, being the son of an evil spirit and a nun. This boy, who was named Merlin, they took to Vortigern, who inquired closely into the stories concerning him. Unafraid, the boy stood before the king. 'Why have you brought me here?' he asked.

Vortigern told him of the wise man's saying, that alone by the death of a boy without a father could the wall be built.

'Your wise man lies to you,' said Merlin. 'Through me, indeed, shall the wall be built: but not through my death. If I speak truly in this, will you give me the heads of your wise men?'

Vortigern was impressed by the boy's bearing and his confident manner, and this he promised to do. Together, Merlin and the king, his wise men and his lords, went to the place where the wall was being built.

Merlin pointed to the fallen stones which lay all around. 'Tell me,' he said to the wise men, 'why does the wall not stand?' But they could not tell him. 'What lies beneath the wall?' Merlin demanded. And again they could not tell him. Merlin turned to the king. 'Beneath this place lies buried a stone, broad and well-hewn. Dig deeper into the earth, King Vortigern, and you shall find it.'

Vortigern ordered his men to dig; and as Merlin had said, they did indeed find a stone slab, broad and well-hewn.

'Wise men,' said Merlin, 'tell me, what lies under this stone?' But they were silent. 'Water lies beneath the stone,' said Merlin. 'Lift it, King Vortigern, and you shall see.'

When the stone was raised, it was as Merlin had said, and a deep pool of dark water lay before them.

'Tell me, if you can, wise men,' said Merlin, 'what lives in this pool.' And again they did not know. Yet Merlin knew. 'In this pool live two dragons, a red and a white. Every night they fight and the earth shakes and thus the wall falls down. Drain away the water and you shall see the dragons.'

When the water had been drained away, it was again as Merlin had said, and out from the place where the pool had been there sprang two dragons, one red and the other white.

They fought together while the king and his men looked on in wonder; but neither dragon could overcome the other, and at last they both sank back into the earth and were never seen again.

'Now keep your promise to me, King Vortigern,' said Merlin. And Vortigern cut off the heads of all his wise men and took Merlin the enchanter to be his only counsellor. Yet Merlin's words were not always welcome to him, for Merlin foretold how, before long, Aurelius and his brother Uther would return to Britain and avenge themselves on the usurper. 'First Aurelius shall be king of Britain,' he said, 'and after him, Uther. But after Uther shall come a greater by far than he: Uther's son, Arthur.'

And it did indeed come to pass as Merlin had said, and before long Aurelius came with Uther and slew Vortigern and ruled as king; but for a short while only. When he was dead his brother Uther was king and leader of the army, and so well he fought against the enemies of Britain, that he brought peace to all the land: yet not until many battles had been fought and won.

Not only against invaders did King Uther have to fight, but also against his own subject, the powerful duke of Cornwall. After they had warred long against each other, the king and the duke made peace, and in token of the peace that was between them, the duke came to Uther's court, bringing with him his wife, the good and beautiful Igraine. There was great merrymaking and rejoicing at court, and much goodwill; but King Uther, who had no queen, fell in love with Igraine. As soon as she learnt of this, Igraine told her husband, counselling him, 'Let us fly from here secretly and return to Cornwall.'

So they took horses and rode all night; and in the morning, when Uther discovered that they were gone, he was angry and sent messengers into Cornwall, commanding the duke to return to court. But this the duke refused to do; so once again there was war between him and the king.

At the head of his knights and men, King Uther rode into Cornwall, and the duke prepared to resist him, shutting himself up in his castle of Terrabil and leaving Igraine to defend his other castle at Tintagel. King Uther laid siege to Terrabil and there was daily fighting between the defenders and the attackers; but after many days the king was no nearer taking Terrabil than he had been at the beginning; and he had little heart in the fighting, for he could think of nothing else but fair Igraine. And so, for love of her, he fell ill and could no longer lead his men.

One of his knights, Ulfius, came to him and said, 'Lord, I shall go to seek Merlin that he may cure your sickness,' and he rode away from the camp. But before he had gone very far he met with Merlin along the road, in the rags of a beggar, and did not know him.

Merlin stopped the knight. 'Whom do you seek?' he asked.

'What is that to you?' asked Ulfius.

Merlin laughed. 'I know that you seek Merlin, and I am he. Go back to the king and say that I am coming.'

Ulfius rode back to the king's pavilion and told him of how he had met Merlin clad like a beggar; and even as he was speaking with the king, Merlin appeared at the entrance to the pavilion.

Uther was glad to see him. 'Can you give me my desire?' he asked eagerly.

'I will give you your desire if, in return, you will give me mine,' replied Merlin.

This the king swore to do. 'What is your desire?' he asked.

'That after you have made Igraine your wife, you will give to me the first child that shall be born to you.'

'You shall have the child,' said Uther.

Then Merlin told the king what he should do to win

Igraine, and forthwith Uther made ready to leave Terrabil and ride with Merlin and Ulfius to Tintagel. But the duke of Cornwall, seeing him about to ride away, and thinking to harass the king's army when its leader was not there, came forth from the castle with a few of his men through a postern gate, and was killed.

Igraine, left a widow, was persuaded to marry the king, and a son was born to them whom they named Arthur; but hardly had they time to rejoice at his birth before Merlin came to ask his reward. King Uther kept his promise and the child, wrapped in cloth of gold, was handed to Merlin, who took him to a good knight named Ector, to be brought up as foster-brother to Kay, Ector's own young son, a year or two older than Arthur.

When a few more years had passed, King Uther fell ill and lay dying. Once again Merlin came to him, and before all the lords gathered there, he asked, 'Is it your will that your son Arthur shall succeed you?'

Uther answered him, 'It is my will.' And soon after, he died.

Immediately King Uther was dead there was great turmoil and trouble in the kingdom, for it was without a ruler, and every lord who thought himself greater than his fellows wished to make himself king. But Merlin caused all the lords and knights to be summoned to London at Christmastide for a tourneying; and when they were come to the city they saw how there stood before the great church a huge stone and an anvil, and wedged fast in the anvil was a sword, and written around the sword in letters of gold were the words: *He who draws forth this sword shall be the rightful king of Britain.*

At once all the lords and knights of Britain who wished to be king, set their hands in turn upon the hilt of the sword and tried to draw it forth from the anvil; but no one of them could so much as stir it.

Now, good Ector had ridden to London for the tourneying, and with him was his son Kay, but newly made knight, and Arthur to serve as Kay's squire. When they reached the tourney-ground on the morning when the contests were to begin, Kay found that in the excitement of setting out for his first jousting, he had forgotten his sword and left it in the inn where they had lodged the night before. 'Quickly, brother,' he said to Arthur, 'ride back to our lodging and fetch me my sword.'

Arthur made haste to do as he was bidden, but when he came to the inn he found the door locked and everyone gone to watch the tourneying. 'I cannot disappoint Kay,' he thought. 'But what shall I do?' Then he remembered the sword which was set in the anvil before the great church, and said to himself, 'My brother Kay shall not be without a sword today. I will pull out the sword from the anvil and take it to him.' He rode swiftly to the churchyard, and seeing no one about, he went to the sword, took hold of the hilt and gave a pull at it. Immediately it came easily out of the anvil. Well pleased, Arthur hastened back to the tourney-ground and gave the sword to Kay.

As soon as Kay saw the sword, he knew it for the one which had been set in the anvil, and he went to his father and said, 'Here is the sword from the anvil, father. Am I then king of Britain?'

'How did you come by it?' asked Ector, astonished.

'Arthur gave it to me.'

Ector sent for Arthur and asked him, 'How did you come by this sword?'

'I pulled it out of the anvil before the church, so that Kay might have a sword.'

'Did any man see you?'

'There was no one there to see me,' said Arthur. 'Have I done wrong?'

Ector looked at Arthur and said slowly, 'Do you know that because of this you must be king of Britain?'

'Why should I be king?' exclaimed Arthur. 'I am no great lord. I am your son and Kay's brother.'

But Ector's only answer was, 'Let me see you replace the sword as you found it, and pull it forth again.'

They went to the great church and there Arthur set the sword back in the anvil, and at once it was held so fast that when Ector tried to draw it forth it would not move, nor would it move for Kay. 'Now let you try,' said Ector; and Arthur set his hand to the hilt and easily pulled the sword forth once again.

Thereupon Ector and Kay knelt down before Arthur, who looked at them in distress. 'My dear father and my brother, do not kneel to me.'

'I am not your father,' said Ector, 'nor is Kay your brother, for you were brought to me as a new-born child by Merlin the enchanter. I do not know who you are, but only that you must be king of Britain.' Arthur wept, for he loved Ector and his wife and Kay. But Ector said, 'When you are king, will you be a good lord to me and my son?'

'How could I be otherwise?' replied Arthur, still weeping.

'I ask no more of you than that you will make my son steward of all your lands.'

'It is such a small request,' said Arthur. 'I shall do it, and more, for him.'

Then Arthur had again to replace the sword in the anvil, and once more, before the lords and subject kings of Britain, to pull it out, after all other men had yet again tried and failed; and so he was proclaimed king of Britain. And Merlin stood forth and declared to everyone that he was the son of Uther and his queen, Igraine. The sword from the anvil Arthur laid as an offering on the altar in the great church, and there in the great church he was first knighted and then crowned. And as he had promised, he made Kay steward of all Britain, and Ulfius he made chamberlain.

Yet there were certain vassals and subject kings in the land who were not content to be ruled by so young an overlord, and they gave Arthur much trouble before, after several years, they were subdued or were won to his side by respect for his achievements.

Arthur was young and fearless, and as ready to fight in single combat as in battle; and he would often ride alone on adventures, challenging any knights whom he encountered or accepting their challenges. In the course of one such adventure Arthur's sword was broken, and as he was making for home, he remarked upon this to Merlin, whom he had met on the road.

'I will find you another sword,' said Merlin. He bade Arthur follow him, and they rode to the edge of a lake and there Arthur, filled with wonder at the sight, saw an arm clothed in white silk rising up from the midst of the water, grasping a sword in a rich scabbard. 'There is the sword,' said Merlin, 'and here is the Lady of the Lake. Speak fairly to her, and she will let you take the sword.'

Astonished, Arthur saw a boat approaching over the water, and in it a lovely maiden. As the boat touched the shore of the lake, the maiden stepped from it, greeting Arthur and Merlin; and they greeted her in return.

'Lady,' said Arthur, 'whose is that sword which the arm holds above the water? For I would it were mine.'

'It is my sword,' she replied. 'Yet I will give it to you as a gift if you wish it. Row out into the lake and take the sword and its scabbard also. They are yours.' And with that she was gone from them.

Arthur and Merlin rowed to the middle of the lake. There Arthur stretched out his hand and took the sword in its scabbard, and immediately the arm sank beneath the water out of sight. They rowed back to the shore, where Arthur eagerly examined the sword, saw how sharp and bright it was, and how its name, Excalibur, was graven on its blade, and he was well pleased with the gift.

When the time came for Arthur to take a wife, he said to Merlin, 'Good friend, advise me in this matter.'

'Is there any maiden whom you would wed sooner than another?' asked Merlin.

'There is indeed,' replied Arthur. 'For I love Guenever, daughter of King Leodegrance.'

Merlin smiled. 'When a man's heart is set on something, he will not easily give it up. It would be useless for me to advise you otherwise than this: send me to King Leodegrance and I will ask Guenever of him for you.'

Leodegrance of Cameliard, one of Arthur's subject kings, was pleased by his request, and gladly gave him Guenever for his wife. And with his daughter he gave to Arthur the Round Table, which Merlin had made for King Uther many years before. This table had places for one hundred and fifty knights, and Arthur gathered about him from all over Britain the best knights that there were in the land, so that in time the noblest, truest and bravest of all men might sit at the Round Table in his court at Camelot – which is now called Winchester. And many are the adventures told of these knights and their gallant deeds.

Arthur had a half-sister – the daughter of Igraine and the duke of Cornwall – named Morgawse, married to King Lot of Orkney, and she was the mother of five sons. At the time of Arthur's marriage she sent Gawaine, the eldest of them, to his uncle's court, where Arthur received him kindly. Gawaine knelt before him. 'My lord uncle,' he said, 'on the day you marry Guenever, will you make me a knight?'

'Willingly,' replied Arthur, pleased by the youth's eagerness. And when the day of his marriage came, he kept his promise, though he did not then guess that Gawaine would, in years to come, be accounted amongst the very best of all his knights.

During the first few years of his reign, Arthur had little peace. He was forced to defend his throne against one after another of those subject kings of Britain who did not wish to acknowledge him as their overlord, and often against foes from beyond the sea. Not long after his marriage he faced a greater danger than any that had so far threatened him. The king of Ireland, the king of Denmark, and three other kings with them, had joined together to conquer Britain and with a mighty army invaded the land, burning and laying waste castles and towns.

When word of this was brought to Arthur, he exclaimed, 'Since I was crowned I have not had a single month of peace. I know I cannot count on all my lords and vassals to follow me against this latest danger, yet – let who will come with me and let who will keep from the fighting – I shall not rest until I have met with these five kings and destroyed them utterly.' Forthwith he called to him his one hundred and fifty loyal knights of the Round Table and bade them make ready with their followers to march against the enemy; and he sent messengers to King Pellinore, one of his loyal vassals, ordering him to come to his help as soon as might be.

But when he came to take leave of Guenever, he could not. 'Lady,' he said, 'I cannot bear the thought of parting from you so soon after our marriage. Come with me, and I swear to you that no harm will befall you, however many our enemies, for your presence will give me strength and greater courage than ever before, and I shall be victorious.'

Guenever smiled at him. 'Lord,' she said, 'I am ready to go with you where you will,' and she made ready to follow him.

Without waiting for King Pellinore to join him, Arthur set out with his small army, Guenever riding beside him, and made for the north, where the five kings were ravaging the land. They reached the River Humber without once encountering the enemy, and this, perhaps, made them less wary than they should have been. On the bank of the Humber they encamped on the edge of the forest land to await the coming of Pellinore, who had made haste to follow Arthur as soon as he had received his summons.

Arthur's foster-brother, Kay, ever cautious and suspicious, said, 'So close to the enemy, it is not safe that we should disarm and sleep.'

But others of Arthur's knights spoke lightly of the danger, and Arthur was persuaded by them and went to rest, together with Guenever, in his pavilion. In a small pavilion close by was young Gawaine, and with him Griflet, a youth who had also but lately been knighted. In the darkness the five kings and their great army fell upon the camp. Arthur was aroused from sleep by the cries and sounds of battle all about him, and almost immediately a wounded knight stumbled into his pavilion calling out, 'The enemy is upon us and our army is destroyed. For the love of heaven, lord, save yourself and the queen.'

In great haste Arthur and Guenever, accompanied by Kay, Gawaine and Griflet, mounted their horses and rode to the river's edge, meaning to cross to the safety of the other side. But they found that the water was too rough and the river too wide for them to pass safely over.

Arthur looked at the dark and rushing stream before him. 'We must choose and choose quickly,' he said. 'If we stay here we shall be taken, and if we are taken we shall undoubtedly be slain; yet if we attempt to cross the river, we may never reach the other bank alive.'

'I would rather die in the water than at the hands of our enemies,' said Guenever. 'Let us attempt the crossing.' Yet the four men hesitated, discussing their chances of success.

'Let us go,' pleaded Guenever. 'We have no time to spare for argument.'

They had less time even than they supposed, for their going had been seen by the five kings as they led their men through the camp to plunder and burn. Calling to each other eagerly, and never waiting for their knights to follow them, the five kings rode alone after Arthur and his companions, loath to miss the chance of capturing or slaying the king of Britain.

While they still hesitated on the brink of the river, Arthur and the others heard the sound of horses' hooves, and straining their eyes against the darkness, made out five knights coming after them. The moonlight glinting on the richness of their armour and on the golden trappings of their mounts showed plainly who they were.

'It is the king of Ireland and the others, and they are alone,' said Kay excitedly. 'Let us turn back and ride against them before any of their men come after them.'

'It would be folly,' said young Gawaine. 'They are five and we are but four, and two of us young and untried.'

'What of that?' said Kay. 'Come, let the three of you take one each, and I will account for the other two.' And with that he turned his horse's head and spurred it on against the pursuers, never waiting to see if Arthur and the others would follow him or no.

The kings, taken by surprise by this sudden, rash attack, were momentarily disconcerted, and Kay's spear passed right through the body of the foremost of them, so that he fell dead from his horse. With shouts of triumph, Arthur and Gawaine rode after Kay, with Griflet close at their horses' heels, and each of them attacked a king. Kay drew his sword and wheeled his horse about to strike at the fifth foe; and a few moments later all the kings lay dead upon the ground.

'That was bravely done,' said Arthur, joyously embracing

Kay. 'All my life I shall remember what you did this night.'

'And I,' said Guenever, 'shall always speak in praise of you, good friend, for it was your courage that saved us.'

Then, all thought of escaping forgotten, Arthur, Kay, Gawaine and Griflet rode back towards their camp, calling out their joyous tidings as they went. All those of Arthur's men who had fled into hiding in the forest, heard him eagerly, and joining with him, followed him back to the camp, impatient to avenge the attack. The enemy had been thrown into confusion by the loss of the five kings, and at dawn was utterly defeated. With the morning came King Pellinore and his army, too late for battle, but in time to share in the rejoicing. When the slain were numbered, it was found that though of the enemy thirty thousand had perished, Arthur had lost no more than two hundred men and eight knights of the Round Table. With this victory Arthur won for himself great honour and the respect of men both in Britain and in the countries over the sea.

Back in Camelot, with peace in the land at last, King Arthur said to Pellinore, 'Tell me, for I value your opinion and your experience, who of all my knights would you consider the most fitted to take the places of those eight who died in battle?'

'Lord,' replied Pellinore, 'you have among your following several older and well-tried knights who would be most worthy of being admitted to the fellowship of the Round Table and I shall name them for you. But first, let places be found for those three young knights who fought so mightily for you against the invaders. Let Kay the steward, Gawaine your nephew and young Griflet be chosen first out of all the others.'

Thus came Kay and Gawaine, young though they were, to join the company of the knights of the Round Table. Kay was always Arthur's loyal friend; and Gawaine soon achieved great renown, both for his courage and his courtesy; and though in time he was joined at court by all his four brothers, he ever remained Arthur's favourite nephew.

Many more adventures King Arthur had, as the years went by, with the fame of his knights spreading far and wide; but in time the noble fellowship of the Round Table was broken. Many knights were lost to Arthur, dead or gone from Britain; and, too, Arthur had lost the good counsel of Merlin, who, for all his wisdom, had fallen into the folly of loving the Lady of the Lake, though she cared nothing for him. Seeking to win her love, he had told her the secrets of his enchantments, and she had learnt them carefully. Then, determined to be rid of him, she had lured him into the cleft of a rock, beneath a great stone, and there she had put a spell on him, so that he remained prisoned fast beneath the stone for all time.

At last there came a day when King Arthur, Gawaine and a great number of their knights with them, went over the sea to fight, and Arthur left Mordred, Gawaine's youngest brother, to rule the land for him. But Mordred had no wish to rule Britain only for a few short months, he longed to be king in Arthur's place; so by a great show of friendship and by promises of rich rewards, he won many knights and lords to his service. He then declared falsely that he had received messages from over the sea telling of Arthur's death, and he had himself crowned king at Canterbury.

Arthur and Gawaine were at the siege of a castle in France when word was brought to them of Mordred's treachery, and they made haste to return to Britain at once. When their ships reached land at Dover, Mordred and his followers were ready waiting for them, and the two armies joined battle fiercely upon the shore. But at the end of the day, though many had fallen on either side, Arthur had gained the advan-

tage, and Mordred fled with all those of his men who still
lived.

When Arthur looked about him to see which of his loyal
knights had died for him in this sad fight of kinsman against
kinsman, he saw Gawaine lying in one of the boats drawn up
upon the beach, wounded and dying. He knelt beside him
and took him in his arms and wept. 'Alas, Gawaine, my good
nephew, you were dearer to me than all my other knights,
and now I must lose you. There shall be no more joy for me
in this life.'

At midday Gawaine died, and Arthur buried him in the
castle at Dover.

Then both Arthur and Mordred gathered their men about
them and marched westward, towards Salisbury, meaning to
have met there in battle on the plain. But the night before
the meeting, as Arthur lay half waking and half sleeping, it
seemed to him that he saw the ghost of Gawaine come to
him, with a great company of fair women. 'You are most
welcome, nephew, for I thought that you were dead,' said
Arthur joyfully. 'Yet tell me, Gawaine, who are these ladies
with you?'

'They are the ladies for whom I fought in righteous causes
during my life, and it is through their prayers that I have
been permitted to come to you tonight to warn you. O my
dear lord, do not give battle to Mordred tomorrow, for if you
do, you will not survive the day. Make peace with him for
one month, until your army is stronger.' And with that it
seemed to the king that Gawaine vanished, and he marvelled
at it.

In the morning Arthur sent two old and trusted knights,
Lucan and his brother Bedivere, to Mordred, to offer him
peace for a month and what lands and goods they thought
well to give.

For his part, Mordred was not sorry to have peace. When

he had heard Arthur's offer, he said, 'I will take Kent and Cornwall now, and be named the king's heir, to have all Britain after him.' And it was agreed that, with no more than fourteen knights each, Arthur and Mordred should meet in the sight of their two armies, drawn up upon the plain, and speak and drink wine together in confirmation of the treaty.

But Arthur had no trust in Mordred's good faith and he bade his men, 'Watch well, and if you see but one sword drawn, come on and strike with all your might, and kill the traitor Mordred and his followers.'

And Mordred, well aware of his base treachery that could not be forgiven, told his men, 'If you see but one sword drawn, come on and strike with all your might, for I have no trust in this treaty. The king means some day to be avenged on me.'

Arthur and Mordred met and spoke of peace between them. Wine was brought and they drank. Then, by misadventure, one of the eight and twenty knights with them, trod upon an adder and it bit him. Looking down, he saw the adder and drew his sword to kill it. Instantly, as they had been bidden, the two armies cried out their defiance and made ready to fight. The trumpets sounded and the battle was begun.

All day the fighting raged, and at evening, as dusk was falling, King Arthur looked around the plain and saw that of all his men, only Lucan and Bedivere were left alive, and they were wounded; and of all Mordred's followers, not one remained.

'That I should have lived to see this day,' grieved Arthur. 'All my good friends save you are gone. And now I, too, have come to my end.' He drew himself up and stared about him. 'I would only that I might have slain that traitor, Mordred.' Then suddenly he caught sight of Mordred, standing a little way off, leaning on his sword, amongst all the dead men.

'Give me my spear,' he said to Lucan, 'for there is the man who is to blame for all this sorrow.'

'Let him be,' said Lucan. 'If he lives, you will have had vengeance enough on him, for his remorse will be most bitter. And remember, lord, the warning of the ghost of Gawaine in the night. In spite of the battle, you yet live. Take no more risks, I beg of you.'

'Whether I live or whether I die,' said Arthur, 'he shall not escape.' He took the spear in both his hands and cried out, 'Traitor, the day of your death is come!' and ran towards Mordred.

Mordred heard his uncle's voice and looked up wearily. Seeing Arthur coming, he straightened himself and lifted his sword and stepped forward. Arthur thrust the point of his spear right through Mordred's body, but Mordred, with all his dying strength, forced himself along the spear shaft until Arthur was within reach of his sword, then he brought the sword down on Arthur's head, cutting through helmet and skull, and the two of them fell together to the ground.

Mordred was dead, but Arthur still lived, though barely; and Lucan and Bedivere, wounded as they were, took him up and carried him from the battlefield to the edge of a nearby lake. But the effort was too much for Lucan, and he died. 'Alas,' said Arthur. 'My good friend, he needed help more than I, yet he did so much for me.'

Bedivere wept for the death of his brother, but Arthur said, 'This is no time for tears. Soon I shall be dead and there is one thing yet which must be done. Take my sword Excalibur and throw it into the water, watching well what there is to see.'

Wondering, Bedivere took the sword and went to the water's edge. But it seemed to him a shame to cast away so good a sword, and he hid it beneath the roots of a tree and returned to Arthur.

'What saw you?' asked Arthur.

'Only the waves and the wind.'

'Then you have not done as I bade you,' said Arthur. 'Go again and do my command.'

Bedivere returned to the water and took the sword from where he had hidden it, but as he raised it to throw it into the lake, he thought again that it could be no good deed to cast away a weapon which had served his king so well, and he hid it once more and went back to Arthur. 'I have done as you bade me,' he said.

'What saw you?' asked Arthur again.

'Only the water lapping and the wind in the waves.'

'You have failed me a second time,' cried Arthur. 'You, whom I have loved and trusted. Do you then covet the sword? Would you steal it for the jewels in the hilt? Go, if you are indeed honourable, and do as I ask.'

Bedivere went a third time to the shore and took up Excalibur and cast it out into the lake. As he did so, an arm came up out of the waves and caught the sword, brandished it three times and vanished with it below the water. Marvelling and afraid, Bedivere returned to the king.

'What saw you?' asked Arthur. And when Bedivere had told him, he said, 'Carry me to the water's edge, for it is time I was gone.'

With difficulty Bedivere carried Arthur to the water, and as they came there, they saw how a barge appeared and came close in by the shore, and in the barge were three queens and the Lady of the Lake, all veiled in black and weeping.

'Lay me in the barge,' said Arthur.

When Bedivere had done so, the barge moved slowly away into the twilight and Bedivere cried out, 'Lord, would you leave me here alone? What will become of me when you are gone?'

'Care for yourself as well as you may, Bedivere, for I can

no longer be of help to you. I go to the Vale of Avalon, to be healed of my wounds, and if you hear of me no more, pray for my soul.'

Bedivere knelt down by the water and wept. Then he arose and in the darkness he stumbled away, knowing and caring not where he went. In the morning he found himself close by a small chapel and a hermitage. Inside the chapel he found the hermit, praying beside a new-made grave. Fearfully he asked, 'Who lies in that grave?'

'Stranger,' replied the hermit, 'last night there came to me certain women who mourned, and they had with them a dead man for whom they asked burial. He it is who lies here.'

'It may well be my lord, King Arthur, who lies in that grave,' said Bedivere. And he remained for the rest of his days with the hermit, praying for the soul of his king. Yet he never knew if it was in truth the body of Arthur which lay in that grave, or whether, as Arthur had himself said, he had gone to the Vale of Avalon to be healed of his wounds and might come again one day to Britain.

And indeed, the end of King Arthur has ever been a mystery. Some say that he is buried near Glastonbury, in a tomb engraved with the words: HIC JACET ARTHURUS, REX QUONDAM REXQUE FUTURUS – *Here lies Arthur, king that was and king to be.* Others say that Arthur and his men are not dead, but that they sleep in a cave, awaiting the day when they are needed to save Britain from her enemies.

*

It is an old tradition that Arthur and his knights are not dead, but sleeping in a cave, and that they will awake to fight again when Britain has need of them. There is a Welsh tale of a shepherd who cut himself a staff from a certain hazel tree growing beside a rock. He then drove his flock to market in London. There a stranger stopped him and told him that if he would lift the rock which lay beside the tree from which he had cut his staff, he would find a vast treasure hidden in a cave beneath the earth. The shepherd hastened home to Wales; raised the rock and entered the cave, where he found the treasure and, guarding it, King Arthur and all his men, fast asleep. The shepherd took up as much treasure as he could carry, but as he was hurrying away with it, he accidentally touched a large bell which hung near the mouth of the cave and it instantly set up a loud clanging. One of the sleepers awoke and asked, 'Is Wales in danger?' 'Not yet,' gasped the terrified shepherd, as the stranger had bidden him answer. The hero went to sleep again and the shepherd came safely out of the cave, vowing he would nevermore set foot in it. But there came a day when his treasure was spent, and the temptation was too much for him: he returned to the cave and once more took up as much gold as he could carry. Again he accidentally set the bell ringing; but when the sleeper stirred and asked, 'Is Wales in danger?' the shepherd did not answer quickly enough, and Arthur and all his men awoke and began to arm themselves. The shepherd dropped his treasure, fled from the cave and never dared to go back there.

The idea of the sleeping warriors who wait with their leader until the day of their country's need, is a familiar one in the folklore of many lands. In the British Isles, a similar tale is told of Finn Mac Cool and his men. But it is said of the Fianna that they will awake not only to save their land, but also if more than a day and a night should pass without the fame of their deeds being mentioned.

Robin Hood

For many years now scholars have been unable to agree over Robin Hood: whether he was indeed a real medieval outlaw who lived in the Nottinghamshire and Yorkshire forests; or whether he was merely a symbolic figure, a mythical King of the Woods who brought luck to the crops and the herds, a faint memory, persisting into the Middle Ages, of the god of some ancient, pre-Christian fertility cult. They will probably go on arguing the point for many years yet.

But is it impossible that he could have been both? There were numberless outlaws in the forestland of medieval England, and there is no reason why one of them, named Robin Hood, should not have achieved local fame and popularity by his daring defiance of authority and his flouting of the harsh laws of his day. He could have become a local legend – perhaps even in his own lifetime; exaggerated accounts of his exploits would have been passed from mouth to mouth; and his fame would not have ended at his death. Indeed, after death he would have increased in might, become more daring, even braver, more resourceful and successful than he had really been. Along with the other fictitious exploits ascribed to him, would come the countrymen's old tales of the wild forests, dim legends transformed through the centuries from those beliefs in some local woodland deity which they must once have been. All these could have combined to make the great body of stories, ballads and traditions concerning that figure which we call Robin Hood.

If it happened that history and myth became inseparably mingled in the case of Arthur, why should it not also be the same in the case of Robin Hood? Though, of course, on a lower social level. Robin, the poor outlaw, cannot compare with the warrior chieftain, leader of an army. Where Arthur became a king, Robin remains a yeoman. Arthur the king and his courteous knights are the heroes of court and castle; Robin Hood with his bunch of jolly, rustic comrades, is the hero of the simple folk, expressing their hopes and aspirations, their longing for freedom, their opposition to authority and their hatred of oppression.

All down the centuries neither Arthur nor Robin Hood has lost his grip on popular imagination. Not only are the old tales in which they figure continually being retold and enjoyed and loved, but even today new stories about them are still being invented.

AT a time when wide forests covered a great part of England, there lived in that wild stretch of land which included Barnsdale Forest in the West Riding of Yorkshire and, immediately south of it, Sherwood Forest near Nottingham, a bold outlaw known as Robin Hood. He came from a yeoman's family and, like many another man in those turbulent days, he had been declared an outlaw for some offence or other and had taken to the forest. There he had soon gathered about him a company of men, who, like himself, were beyond the law, and in the manner of other bands of outlaws all over England, they robbed travellers riding through the forest and lived happily and safely in the greenwood. Yet, unlike other robbers, Robin and his men did no harm to the peasants and the farmers, and for the sake of the Blessed Virgin they molested no women who passed through the forest, but showed them all respect and courtesy; and much of what they took from the rich, they gave to the poor. However, Robin Hood hated the rich churchmen, all those who were greedy and corrupt, and he stole from them whenever he might; and he waged ceaseless strife against the harsh Sheriff of Nottingham, whom he considered his greatest enemy.

Among Robin's men were his cousin, Will Scarlet, Little John – so called in jest for his huge size, Much, the son of a miller, and Friar Tuck, the Curtal Friar of Fountain Dale, who had been cast forth by his prior and brethren for his unruly ways, and had come to the forest, where he sang masses for the outlaws under the green branches of the trees.

Robin Hood never refused his help or the help of his men in a worthy cause. One who benefited greatly by the outlaw's generosity was Sir Richard of the Lea, and this is how it came about.

It was ever Robin's wont, before the midday meal, to hear three masses, one of the Father, one of the Holy Spirit and one of Our Lady, whom Robin considered his particular protectress and patron. One morning midday was fast approaching and Robin had not yet given word for the first mass to be said, but was standing thoughtfully, leaning against a tree, with Little John, Will Scarlet and Much the miller's son near by him.

Little John, who was growing hungry, said 'It is time you thought of eating, master. To my mind, you have fasted long enough.'

Robin looked at him with a smile. 'I am in no haste to eat, though I do not doubt that you are. So go quickly and find a guest to eat with us, to make us merry and, perhaps, to pay well for his entertainment, if his purse is fat enough.'

'What manner of guest, master?'

'What you will, Little John. Knight, squire or abbot, it is all one to me. Go you up to Watling Street with Will and Much and bring me the first man whom you see.'

So the three outlaws went to the old road which ran

through the forest, and before long they saw a solitary knight riding towards them along the track, his head bent and his face sorrowful. They called out to him, and he reined in his horse.

'My master, Robin Hood, bids you dine with him in the greenwood, stranger,' said Little John.

The knight's face lightened for a moment. 'I have heard much good of Robin Hood, for all he is an outlaw and a robber. Willingly shall I dine with him.'

They led him to Robin, who greeted him kindly; and when they had heard the three masses, they all sat down in the shade of the forest trees to eat good venison and game and to drink stolen wine. The strange knight ate and drank, and he talked courteously enough to them, but it was plain that he had some trouble on his mind, though he made no mention of it.

When the meal was over, Robin said, 'Now, sir knight, if you consider the entertainment worthy of your rank, perhaps you would be willing to pay for it, since it is unfitting that a yeoman should be charged with the cost of a knight's meat.'

The knight flushed and looked away. 'In the coffer at my saddlebow I have but ten shillings,' he said quietly. 'Take it, if you think it enough, for I have no more.'

'If that is all you have,' said Robin, 'I would wish rather to give, than to take from you.' And he bade Little John open the knight's coffer.

'It is true, master. There is no more than ten shillings,' said Little John, tipping the money on to the grass from the coffer.

Robin turned to the stranger. 'How comes a knight of your standing to have no more than ten shillings in his coffer?'

The knight was silent for a moment, then he said, 'My name is Richard of the Lea. I have a son of twenty years old.

Some months past, in fair fight he slew a knight of Lanca-
shire and his squire. This knight had powerful kinsfolk who
are no friends to me, and so my son was taken and cast into
prison. To save him from a shameful death, I gave all the gold
I owned – and more beside, for I pledged my lands to the
abbot of St Mary's Abbey in York. I have now no money to
redeem them, so I am on my way to beg the abbot to allow
me a longer time in which to pay him. Yet I have no hope
that he will hear me. He is a hard man.' The knight sighed
and fell silent, staring at the ground.

'What sum do you owe to the abbot?' asked Robin.

'Four hundred pounds.'

'You shall not go to him empty-handed,' said Robin, and
he called to Little John to fetch him four hundred pounds
from the outlaws' money chests. When the gold had been
counted out, Robin asked, 'What surety can you give me for
my loan?'

The knight shook his head sadly. 'None. In the days of my
prosperity I had friends enough. They are my friends no
longer. Not one of them would speak for me.'

Robin shrugged. 'You can hardly expect me to lend my
good gold without a surety.'

'I have told you : I can offer you no surety. I have no friend
left save Our Lady. She has always been good to me, and will
not desert me now.'

'Our Lady !' exclaimed Robin. He sprang to his feet laughing. 'I would take her bond for any sum. Come, gather up
the money and put it in your coffer and I will expect you
here a twelvemonth from today to repay the loan.'

Sir Richard looked on bewildered by his good fortune as
the coins were counted into his coffer; but Little John whispered to Robin, 'Master, his clothes are threadbare and
shabby. It is unseemly for a knight to travel so. Let me find
him a surcoat and a cloak.'

Robin nodded, and Will Scarlet, standing near, said, 'And a pair of boots. Look at his own. His toes will be worn through before he reaches York.'

So they gave Sir Richard new, bright garments and a pack-horse to carry the gold. Then Robin said, 'It is not fitting that a knight should ride unattended, nor is it wise that a man should face the abbot of St Mary's without a friend at his side. Take Little John with you as your squire, if you will.'

Joyfully Sir Richard of the Lea thanked Robin Hood, mounted his horse and rode off with Little John towards York.

On the morning of the following day, the abbot of St Mary's Abbey in York sat at meat with the more important of the brethren, and with his guest, the Lord Chief Justice, beside him. 'A year ago this day,' he said with satisfaction, 'I lent four hundred pounds to Sir Richard of the Lea. Unless he pays it back today, all his lands are mine.'

The prior, a good and kindly man, looked up and said quickly, 'It is still early in the day. He has until midday to repay the loan. His lands are not yet yours.'

'Today is the day we named and he has not come. His good lands shall be mine, without a doubt,' said the abbot.

'He is a worthy knight,' said the prior. 'It is a shame that he should be so wronged. I would give one hundred pounds of my own, that I might spare him this. God send he may yet come in time.'

The fat, red-faced cellarer chuckled. 'Your worthy knight, he is dead or hanged. He will not come.'

'I, too,' said the Lord Chief Justice, 'doubt that he will come, or he would be here by now.'

But they were mistaken, for at that very moment Sir Richard and Little John were being admitted by the porter. Leaving Little John outside with the money and the horses,

Sir Richard went alone into the hall, and going to the abbot, knelt before him, greeting him courteously.

When the abbot saw who it was, he frowned and without another word he demanded, 'Where is my money?'

Looking up at him and seeing the greed on his face and the spite in his mean little eyes, Sir Richard was minded to test the abbot. 'I have not brought it,' he said. 'I have come to beg you for a longer time in which to repay the loan.'

'You have had time enough. You will get no more.'

Sir Richard looked about him and saw the Lord Chief Justice. 'Good sir justice, be my friend and speak for me,' he pleaded.

'You have lost your lands,' said the Lord Chief Justice, 'if you do not repay the loan today.'

Sir Richard turned again to the abbot. 'Good abbot, have pity on me. Do not take my lands and I will be a true servant to you and to your monastery until I have paid you all I owe.'

The abbot grew angry. 'I swear by God that you shall never have back your lands from me. So leave my hall, false knight.'

'I was never a false knight,' said Sir Richard quietly. Then he rose to his feet. 'It is discourteous of you to leave a knight kneeling before you for so long.' He went to the door of the hall and called to Little John, who came in with the coffer. Sir Richard took the coffer to the table, and opening it, poured out the gold upon the table top. 'Take your money, sir abbot. My Lord Chief Justice here and your monks are all witnesses that I have repaid you in full and may keep my lands.' And with that he turned and walked from the hall, followed by Little John, who was grinning fit to split his face in two.

Beyond York they parted, and Sir Richard hastened home to tell his anxious wife his joyous news; while Little John made his way back to Robin Hood and his comrades, with a merry tale to tell them.

When the twelve months were over and the day had come round when Sir Richard of the Lea was due in the greenwood to pay his debt to Robin Hood, the outlaws awaited him in the place where he had dined with them before. But the morning passed and midday came and went and there was no sign of Sir Richard. A frown appeared on Robin's brow and he grew solemn. 'I would have sworn that knight was true,' he said. 'It must be that Our Lady is angered with me for some cause, and so does not restore me my money.'

'He will come, master, never doubt,' said Little John. 'There is still time; the day is not yet done. But will you not sit down and eat and drink? That way the time will pass less slowly and the waiting will be less wearisome.'

Robin sighed. 'Very well, let us eat. But since I have been cheated of the guest whom I expected, let me at least have another guest to eat with me in his place. Go up to Watling Street with Much and Will Scarlet and bring me the first man you see, whether he be lord, peasant or churchman, and he shall dine with us today.'

So once again, as they had done a year before, the three outlaws went to the road that ran through the forest and waited to see who would come by. In a very short time there came in sight two monks riding ahead of a number of men-at-arms and servants leading seven well-laden packhorses.

Little John counted the men. 'Two and fifty of them. By the saints, these monks ride as royally as any bishop. I warrant they have brought our pay in those packs of theirs.'

'There are but three of us,' said Much doubtfully.

Little John laughed. 'Robin will hardly be pleased with us if we do not bring him his guest. Have your arrows ready, my friends.'

They waited until the cavalcade was almost abreast of

them, and then stepped out on to the track, the three of them each with an arrow fitted to his bow, right in the path of the monks.

'Wait!' Little John called out. 'You shall go no further, you two monks. Would you keep my master any longer from his meat?'

One of the two monks, with a fat, red face, reined in his horse and timidly held back; but the other demanded angrily, 'And who may your master be, you impudent knave?'

'My master,' replied Little John, 'is Robin Hood.'

'I have heard much of him,' exclaimed the monk furiously. 'A great rogue and a thief he is. Out of my way, you scoundrels!' And he urged forward his horse as though he would have ridden down the three outlaws.

Much let fly an arrow and shot him through the heart. He fell from his horse, and all the men-at-arms, fearing that it was an ambush and that they were about to be slain, turned their mounts and fled, and the serving-men with them, leaving the packhorses and the other monk to fend for themselves. With glee the three outlaws led their booty and their prisoner to Robin Hood, who greeted the terrified monk courteously enough and bade him say mass for them, so that they might sit down and eat.

When mass was done and the food and drink had been brought, Robin put his unwilling guest in the place of honour and served him with meat and wine himself. 'Where is your home, sir monk?' he asked.

'I come from St Mary's Abbey in York. I am the cellarer.'

'You are well met,' said Robin. 'Our Lady was surety for a loan which I made to a good knight a twelvemonth ago. Today the loan was to be repaid. Since you come from her abbey, I have no doubt that Our Lady has sent me the money by you.'

'I know nothing of what you speak,' said the monk hastily.

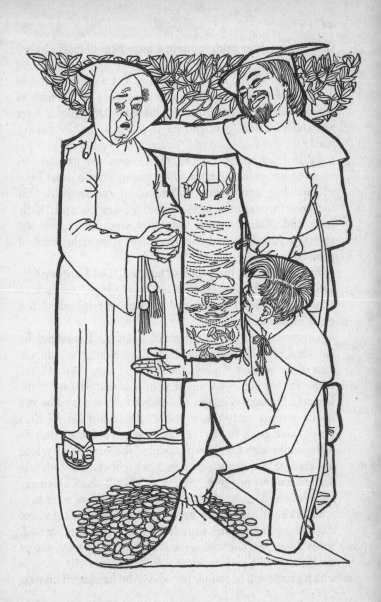

'I have no money with me save a mere twenty marks in my coffers.'

'If that is all you have,' said Robin, 'not a penny of it will I take. Indeed, I shall give you some money of my own to see you safely home to York.' He turned to Little John. 'Open the coffers, Little John, and see if you can find the twenty marks.'

Little John spread out his cloak upon the ground and emptied one coffer after another into it, until a great heap of gold lay before them, glittering in the sunlight that flickered through the trees. When it was counted, Little John said, 'Our Lady has not failed you, master. She has returned your loan and doubled it. Here are eight hundred pounds.'

Robin looked at the gold and laughed. 'Did I not say Our Lady was the best surety any man could have? Go back to your abbot, master monk, and tell him to send me such a guest for dinner every day.'

The cellarer needed no second bidding. Trembling, he mounted his horse and hastened off, the laughter and the jeers of the outlaws ringing in his ears.

Hardly was the monk out of sight when Sir Richard of the Lea came himself with a small band of followers, and he and Robin greeted each other gladly. But when Sir Richard would have given Robin the four hundred pounds which he had brought with him in repayment of the loan, Robin would not take it. 'No, my friend, keep your money. Our Lady has already sent me my gold.' And he told Sir Richard about the cellarer of St Mary's Abbey and his eight hundred pounds.

Sir Richard laughed to hear how the hard-hearted abbot had lost eight hundred pounds in good gold, then he said, 'Even if you will not take my money, you will, I trust, accept the gift which I have brought you. It is a poor gift, but one which I hope will be found welcome.' And he ordered his men to bring his gift – one hundred fine new bows and one hundred sheaves of peacock-feathered arrows.

Robin was well pleased with this gift. He grasped Sir Richard's hand and said, 'Now you must allow me to make you a gift in return. Little John, bring me half of the money which Our Lady sent me today, for I would share it with my good friend here.'

So as well as his own four hundred pounds, which he had thought to leave with Robin, Sir Richard rode home to his wife with another four hundred pounds, after many a promise of friendship and of his help if ever the outlaws were in need of it.

Robin Hood and his men were to need Sir Richard's help far sooner than they could have dreamt. For it happened, not long after, that the Sheriff of Nottingham proclaimed a shooting match for all the archers in the district, the prize for the winner to be an arrow of silver, tipped and feathered with gold. Robin and a number of his men were at that time in Sherwood Forest, close by Nottingham town.

'What say you, my friends, shall we go and see this shooting and maybe take a part in it?' asked Robin eagerly; and there was not one of those with him who did not wish to go.

At the contest they found many a good archer trying his skill, but none was more skilled than the best of Robin's men. And there was not one of Robin's men – not even Little John or Will Scarlet, good archers though they were – who could beat their master, for Robin Hood excelled all men in shooting. So that in the end it was not surprising that it was Robin who won the prize.

His men stood close together for safety and gripped their bows ready to shoot again – and not for any prize this time – as Robin went up to the stand where the sheriff sat with his lady and his friends, to receive the silver arrow.

At first it seemed as though all would be well, but just as Robin was turning away to go back to his men, someone near the sheriff cried out, 'By all the saints, it is Robin Hood the outlaw!'

Robin did not wait a moment to deny it. He leapt down from the stand and ran towards his men. Yet neither did the sheriff waste a moment. He called out to his men-at-arms, bidding them shoot down the outlaws and their leader. But Robin's men were ready, and it was their arrows which were loosed first, wounding several of the sheriff's men. Then, with Robin, they made haste to the edge of the contest ground and were away on the road leading to the forest, with a crowd of terrified spectators in between them and the sheriff's followers. Their readiness had given them an advantage, but it did not last for long. Before they had gone very far along the road, the sheriff's men-at-arms had thrust a way through the crowd and were once again shooting. The outlaws shot back at them: and their arrows had a truer aim. Alternately running as fast as they might in the direction of the forest, and turning to stand long enough to shoot back at their pursuers, they made their way towards the forest and safety.

All might have gone well for them had an arrow not struck Little John in the knee. Much the miller's son heaved him up and slung him over his shoulder – not without difficulty, for Little John was no light weight – and they went on. But there was no more running for them after that, for Much, staggering and stumbling along, could hardly even walk with his burden. Yard by yard they fought their way to the shelter of the forest, but every step of the way the sheriff's men were gaining on them.

'We shall never reach the forest alive, Robin,' gasped Will Scarlet. He pointed. 'Not half a mile that way lies good Sir Richard's castle. He would give us help. What say you, shall we go to him?'

And though Robin was loath to bring trouble upon Sir Richard, he knew it was their only hope, and he called out to the others to make their way to the little castle which stood on the very edge of the forest-land, with a good wall and a ditch around it.

Sir Richard of the Lea, seeing from the ramparts the commotion on the track that led to his home, was ready for them with his drawbridge down, and hardly were they safely within his walls and the drawbridge raised again, than the sheriff's men-at-arms – with the sheriff himself on a horse now joined with them – were clamouring from beyond the moat, demanding that the outlaws should be given up to them. But Sir Richard, overjoyed to have been of service to Robin and his comrades, was too busy making them welcome and tending Little John's wound, to pay any heed to the sheriff's demands; and after a time, the sheriff, very angry, rode back to Nottingham, followed by his disappointed men.

The outlaws remained in Sir Richard's castle for only a few days, and then they were away to the forest once more, leaving Little John to stay for a week or so longer, until he could walk again.

But meantime the sheriff rode to London to tell the king of how Sir Richard of the Lea was aiding the outlaws from the forest and setting at naught all the laws of the land. The king promised to come himself within a fortnight to arrest the knight and to put down the outlaw band, and he bade the sheriff return at once to Nottingham and call together as many men-at-arms as he could muster to be ready for his coming.

However, the sheriff was impatient and still angry, and he lay in wait for Sir Richard one day when, believing all was safe and peaceful once again, the knight rashly rode out hawking. Triumphantly, the sheriff took him and led him bound to Nottingham.

Sir Richard's wife, in great distress, mounted a palfrey and herself rode with all speed to the forest to find Robin Hood and tell him of what had befallen. With tears she said, 'I beg of you, do not leave him to die a shameful death.'

In an instant Robin had called together his men and bade them arm themselves. 'Never fear, lady,' he said, 'I promise you, we shall save our good friend.' And in no time at all they were on their way to Nottingham, more than seven score of them.

In the streets of Nottingham they met with the sheriff's men, with the sheriff at their head; and while the townsfolk locked themselves up in their houses and trembled, the outlaws and the men-at-arms fought in the narrow streets. By the end of that day's fighting, the sheriff lay dead with Robin's arrow through his heart, and Sir Richard was free and riding for the forest with Robin and his men.

In two weeks' time, as he had promised, the king came with a goodly following of knights and squires, and a large troop of men-at-arms, to take Sir Richard and Robin Hood. But however far into the forest he went in search of the outlaws, they were always deeper yet in the wild woodland, and he could never catch a sight of even one of them. But all the time, just in that part of the forest where he was not, they would be poaching his deer, and every day word would be brought to him by his foresters of how Robin merely laughed at him and at the royal men-at-arms, and took game where he would. Until at last it seemed to the king that, even with a much greater force at his command, he never would catch Robin Hood, and he said as much.

An old forester who was standing near made bold to speak to him. 'That is as may be, sire. But if you would have sight of Robin Hood, free and among his own loyal men, I can show you a way to do it.'

The king turned at once to the forester. 'If I may not catch him, I may at least see him before I ride back to London. Tell me, how shall it be done?'

'Choose out your five best knights, sire, and no more than them. Let you all put on the garb of monks and I will lead you into the forest, and I warrant that before long you will have sight of Robin Hood.'

Several there cried out against the danger of such an undertaking, fearing it to be a trap; but the king's eyes grew bright and he threw back his head and laughed, for he ever loved jests, and this promised to be a rare one. 'We shall do as you say, forester. Let us make ready at once.' And he chose out five knights to go with him.

Not long after this a small group rode out from Nottingham; the king first, in the guise of an abbot, his cowl pulled well forward about his face, and his five knights after him, looking as much like the abbot's meek and reverent monks as they might; while in front of them plodded the old forester, to lead them on their way. On they went along the forest path where all about them the woods seemed quiet and sleeping in the afternoon sunlight; and then suddenly before them on the track there was a small band of men clad all in green. Their leader laid his hands upon the bridle of the king's horse and looked up at him, smiling.

'By your leave, sir abbot,' said Robin, 'I would hold you here with us for a while. A bare living we in the greenwood gain by killing the king's deer: you have rents from your abbey lands and your church coffers are filled with gold. Of your charity, sir abbot, give us some money to spend.'

With his face shadowed by his cowl, the king looked carefully at Robin, then he said, 'I have been at Nottingham for the past fortnight with our lord the king, and great expense have I had feasting all his lords and knights. I have but forty pounds remaining.'

'It will be enough,' said Robin, holding out his hand.

The king untied the bag of gold from his saddlebow and held it in his hand for a moment while he watched Robin. Then he chuckled. 'I believe that if it were one hundred pounds I would not be sorry to give it to you.' He dropped the bag into Robin's outstretched palm.

Robin opened the bag and counted out the money. Then he handed twenty of the gold pieces to Much who stood beside him. 'That is for the men to make merry on,' he said. The other twenty pieces he returned to the bag, drew the thongs tightly about its neck and handed it back to the king. 'That is for your expenses until you reach home. And now, my lord abbot, I should be well pleased if you would dine with me.'

The king bent his head. 'I shall be honoured to be your guest.'

Robin led the way to a spreading oak tree and there he blew a single blast upon his horn, and instantly all his men came running towards the great tree, all seven score of them. The king, seeing them, smiled wryly and murmured half bitterly to that one of his knights who was nearest to him, 'His men come at his bidding more willingly than my men come at mine.'

Meat and drink were brought: roasted venison, huge loaves of bread, good red stolen wine, and strong brown ale; the king was seated in the place of honour and Robin himself served him.

'Now, sir abbot,' said Robin when the meal was over, 'if you would see our skill with the bow, willingly shall we display it, and you may tell our lord the king of our life in the greenwood, when next you speak with him.'

The ground was paced out and the targets – white-peeled hazel wands hung with garlands of wild roses – were set up while the king looked on. 'The targets are too far away by fifty paces,' he said.

Robin shook his head. 'I think not, sir abbot. I know the skill of my men.' He laughed. 'If anyone fails to send his arrows through the garland, I shall box his ears myself.' All his men, standing about him, laughed with him and made ready to shoot.

They shot in turn, one after the other and three arrows each; and there were but few of all the seven score who failed to send each of their three arrows through the garland. Those few who did fail, Robin, laughing, clouted, and they laughingly took the blow.

The king, watching eagerly, marvelled. 'Your archers are far better than the king's, my friend,' he said to Robin.

Then, when it came last of all to Robin's turn, with his two first arrows he not only shot through the garland of roses, but he split two of the thin hazel wands. Yet by an unlucky chance his third arrow failed even to pass through the garland by more than three fingers' breadth. 'The devil must have guided that arrow!' he exclaimed. All his men laughed, but none more heartily than Robin himself. He turned to the king. 'I have earned myself a buffet by my bad marksmanship, sir abbot. Will you not give it to me?'

'I should be loath to strike a kindly host,' smiled the king.

'Strike on boldly,' laughed Robin.

'As you will,' said the king and, rising, he rolled up the sleeve of his monkish habit and gave Robin a blow that sent him staggering with its unexpected strength.

'You have a fine fist for a churchman. I warrant you could shoot far and straight.' Robin grinned; and then the smile died on his lips and he stared at the supposed abbot, whose cowl, as he struck the blow, had fallen back from his head to show his long, golden-brown hair. 'You are no monk,' said Robin slowly.

Sir Richard of the Lea gave a gasp. 'It is our lord the king.' He dropped to his knees. 'I know, for I have seen him before.'

Robin knelt down and all his men did likewise, fearfully, wondering what would befall them. 'Have mercy on us all, sire,' said Robin.

The king stood there silently for a few moments, looking about him at the men who knelt before him. Then he smiled. 'Your skill is wasted here in the forest. I would have such men as you my friends. You shall be pardoned every one, and free to return to your own homes.' He turned to Robin. 'And you, Robin Hood, I would have you take service with me, if you will.'

Robin rose, came closer and knelt again before the king and kissed his hand. 'I thank you for your great goodness, sire. I will be loyal to you,' he promised.

So Robin went to court to serve the king; yet not for long, for before many years were past there was another king in England and Robin was back in the forest again with many of his former comrades, enjoying the old free life of an outlaw. And thus he and his friends lived for many years, shooting the king's deer, stealing from the rich churchmen, giving the fruits of their thefts to the poor, and always showing respect and courtesy to all women.

Yet for all the honour that he ever paid them, it was a woman who betrayed Robin Hood to his death at the last.

He had a cousin, Ursula, who was abbess of a convent at Kirklees, in Yorkshire, and she was famed for her skill in medicine and all manner of herbs and simples. Falling sick of an old wound, Robin determined to go to Kirklees that Dame Ursula might heal him by her remedies. He sent word to her that he was coming and set off, accompanied only by Little John. But for the sake of her friendship with a knight, Sir Roger of Doncaster, who had hated Robin for many years, she promised to kill him when he came.

At Kirklees, leaving Little John to wait for him beyond the

walls, Robin went secretly to the convent door and Dame Ursula let him in. She took him to a little room and bade him lie down upon the bed. Then she gave him a draught which she said would ease his pain, and told him that she would bleed him.

Robin smiled at her. 'I thank you, good cousin, for all your kindness,' he said wearily.

But the draught she had given him was drugged, so that he fell into a heavy sleep, and while he slept she cut deeply into his wrist with her knife and left him alone, with the blood dripping steadily from his arm into a silver bowl.

Hours later Robin awoke. He was weak and faint, and when with an effort he raised his head, he saw how the bowl beside the bed was filled to the brim and how the bright red blood still dripped from his wrist; and he knew he had been betrayed. With all the little strength that remained to him he dragged himself from the bed and bent to take up his horn which he had laid beside him on the floor, together with his bow and quiver. But the effort was too much for him and he fell. Yet, undaunted, he took hold of his horn, and drawing it after him over the floor, crawled slowly across the room to the narrow little window. There he pulled himself upright, and setting the horn to his lips, blew one faint blast – all he had the strength for. Yet faint as it was, Little John, waiting beyond the walls, heard it and started up, thinking, 'What ails Robin that he blows so weakly?' and ran for the convent gate.

He terrified the old portress into admitting him, then, finding the house door closed against him, he broke the lock and stormed from room to room through the convent, while the frightened nuns ran before him, until he found the room where Robin lay by the window. Little John went to him and raised him gently in his arms. Robin opened his eyes and smiled at him. 'I knew that you would come,' he whispered.

'But you are almost too late, for all that.' He closed his eyes again.

'I shall come back,' said Little John, 'with all your men, and we shall burn Kirklees Convent, every stick and stone of it, and all the nuns in it. Never fear, you will be avenged, master.'

Robin opened his eyes again. 'We have never yet harmed a woman. Would you begin the moment I am not there to forbid you? Let the nuns be.' He struggled to rise. 'Now help me up, Little John, and bring me my bow from beside the bed. I have a mind to shoot my last arrow. Where it falls, bury me there.'

Little John put bow and arrow into his hands, then held him up while Robin, hardly strong enough to bend the bow, took aim. Out of the window sped the arrow and over the convent wall, into the grass beside the highway. Robin smiled once more at his old friend, then the bow slipped gently from his hands and he fell back into Little John's supporting arms.

Where the arrow had fallen the outlaws buried Robin Hood below the green grass; and there was not one of them all that did not weep for him.

*

Robin Hood is popularly associated with the latter half of the twelfth century, and the king who visited him in Sherwood Forest is usually held to have been Richard I. But the staunchest of the supporters of the authenticity of Robin Hood as a real historical figure can offer a number of good reasons for his having lived at the very end of the thirteenth and the beginning of the fourteenth centuries. In this case, the king in question will be Edward II. If one accepts the story of the meeting between king and outlaw in Sherwood Forest as a historical fact, and not as one of the many fictions which grew up around the name of Robin Hood, then the king is more likely to have been Edward than Richard. Edward II ruled for twenty years, and in that time was away from his country for no more than a few weeks in all. Richard I, that greatest of all absentee landlords, spent no more than twelve months in England out of a ten-year reign. During the November of 1323, Edward passed more than a fortnight at Nottingham. In the king's household expenses account for the following year, between April and November, there are several entries for payments made to one 'Robyn Hod' or 'Robert Hood' – the name is variously spelt, after the fashion of the times – who was then in the king's service. The king's comment that the outlaw's men come more willingly at their master's bidding than his own men come at his, better fits Edward, whose barons were always at variance with him, than Richard, to whom his 'men' would have meant his crusading soldiers, who both loved and respected their leader. One may add to that, that Edward II, who took pleasure in simple amusements and liked simple folk, would surely have thoroughly enjoyed the fun of dressing up as a monk and going off incognito to meet a bunch of outlaws.

WALES

Pwyll and Rhiannon

There are a number of fine tales among the old Welsh legends. Since they were all written down in the form in which we now have them, after the coming of Christianity, the heroes and heroines of these stories are mere mortals: kings and queens and princes and enchanters, certainly, but no more than that. Yet, in their earliest forms, these tales will have been the myths of the ancient British deities, the gods and goddesses of those Celts who settled in these islands before the Romans came.

AT that time when Pwyll was prince of Dyved, he was one day keeping his court at Narberth. Close by the castle stood a small hill. 'Lord,' said someone to Pwyll, 'it is said that if a man sit upon that hill, he will either receive a wound or a blow, or he will see a marvel.'

'Among so many good friends,' smiled Pwyll, 'I need have no fear of wounds or blows. But a marvel I would gladly see.' So he went and sat upon the top of the hill and waited.

After a time he saw a young woman, clothed in shining gold and riding on a white palfrey, coming slowly towards the hill. 'Is there any amongst you who knows this lady?' Pwyll asked his followers. But there was no one of them all who knew her. 'Let one of you go and meet her and ask her name,' ordered Pwyll.

One of his men rose and went down to the road at the foot

of the hill, and as he stepped on to the road, the lady came by on her horse. He called out to her, but she did not stop, and he went after her. Yet, though she had seemed to be riding slowly as she approached, when he came to go after her, he found that her speed was such that he had to run to equal it; and yet even so, he could not catch up with her. And the faster he ran, the farther away from him she was. So that at last, out of breath, he had to give up the chase and return to Pwyll.

'Go back to the castle, fetch the swiftest horse in the stables and follow her,' Pwyll commanded him.

The young man did so; but the faster he rode, the farther away appeared the lady on her white palfrey. And in the end his horse could carry him no longer and he had to return again to Pwyll. 'Lord,' he said to him, 'it is useless to follow her.' And he explained how matters stood.

'Truly,' said Pwyll eagerly, 'I think this may be a marvel. Let us come here again tomorrow.'

Accordingly, the next day Pwyll went a second time with the same companions to the top of the little hill and they took with them a swift horse, to be ready should the lady come again. And indeed, they had hardly sat down to wait before she came in sight, riding slowly on her white palfrey. 'Away and after her,' said Pwyll to one of the young men, and the young man mounted and rode along the highway. But it happened the same as on the day before. Whenever he thought to overtake her, she seemed farther from him; and though he spurred his horse along the road after her, he could not come up with her; and at last he gave up the chase and returned to Pwyll.

'Tomorrow,' said Pwyll, 'we shall come again to this hill, and tomorrow I shall ride after the lady myself, for truly, this is indeed a marvel.'

On the third day it went as it had gone before: the lady

came in sight and went along the road at the foot of the hill, and this time Pwyll mounted hastily and rode after her. It seemed to him that he should easily come up with her, for she was riding slowly, but the faster he went, the farther away she appeared. And though he urged on his horse to its greatest speed, he was no nearer to her than at first. At last he called out, 'Lady, wait for me.'

Immediately she reined in the white palfrey, calling back to him, 'Willingly shall I wait for you. It would have been kinder to your horse had you asked me sooner.' She threw back the veil which covered her face and smiled at him, so that Pwyll thought she was the most beautiful maiden he had ever seen. 'Lady,' he asked, 'what is your errand?'

'I came to seek you, prince of Dyved,' she replied.

'No errand could have pleased me better,' said Pwyll, overjoyed. 'Will you not tell me your name?'

'I am Rhiannon, the daughter of Heveydd Hen, and I have come to seek you because my father would give me in marriage to a man I do not love. It is you I love, Pwyll, and if you will not have me, then I shall live unwed.'

'If I had all the ladies in the world to choose from,' said Pwyll, 'I would choose you for my wife.'

'Then if you would marry me before I am given to another,' said Rhiannon, 'come to my father's house this day twelvemonth, and I will see that a feast is prepared for you.'

'I will come,' he promised her; and they parted.

Pwyll kept silent about all that had passed between him and Rhiannon; but when a year had gone by, he set out with a hundred followers to the house of Heveydd Hen to ask for the hand of his daughter. Heveydd Hen welcomed him gladly, and as Rhiannon had promised, a great feast had been prepared for him. At the height of the feasting, as Pwyll was sitting with Rhiannon on one side of him and her father on the other, a tall, auburn-haired young man came into the hall and greeted Pwyll and his companions.

'You are welcome, stranger,' said Pwyll. 'Come, sit and eat with us.'

But the young man shook his head. 'I will not sit and eat, lord,' he said, 'for I am here but to ask a boon of you.'

Rhiannon laid her hand on Pwyll's arm, but he did not look at her, and before she could prevent him, he had replied cheerfully, 'Ask your boon, my friend, and if it is anything which I can grant, willingly shall I grant it.'

'Why did you give him such an answer?' cried Rhiannon.

The stranger smiled. 'The answer has been given before many witnesses,' he said.

'Come,' said Pwyll, 'tell me the boon, that I may grant it.'

'All I ask is this,' said the young man, 'that you give me your place at this feast, and that you give me your bride, for I have long loved her.'

Pwyll sat silent, staring at the young man; but Rhiannon said bitterly to him, 'Small use have you made of your wits tonight. This is Gwawl, to whom I was to have been married against my will. Now you must keep your promise or be shamed for ever.'

'Rhiannon,' said Pwyll, 'I cannot give you up to him.'

'You must do so,' she said. Then she lowered her voice and urged him, 'Give me up to him, as you have promised. Yet refuse him the feast, and I will never be his bride. Only trust me, and all will yet be well.'

'I am waiting for your answer, Pwyll,' said Gwawl.

'And here it is,' said Pwyll. 'All that is mine to give, I give you. My bride is yours. Yet the feast is not mine to give.'

'I and my father,' said Rhiannon, 'have given this feast to the men of Dyved and to our own men. We cannot take it from them. Come back this day twelvemonth, Gwawl, and

we shall hold a feast for you and your men, and I shall be your bride that day.'

Gwawl left the house of Heveydd Hen well pleased; but Rhiannon gave Pwyll a small sack, and told him what he must do with it. Then he, too, went away.

When a year was passed, Gwawl came to claim his bride, and a great feast was prepared for him and his men in the house of Heveydd Hen. And Pwyll came also, with his hundred followers, and waited outside the house, in the orchard. And when the feasting was at its highest, Pwyll, clad like a beggar, even as Rhiannon had bidden him, and carrying the sack which she had given him, came into the hall and greeted the company.

'You are welcome,' said Gwawl. 'Heaven bless you.'

'Lord,' said Pwyll, 'I would ask a boon of you.'

'Ask it, stranger, and if it is a fair boon, I will grant it.'

'It is only that you will fill with food this bag I carry, lord, that I may take it away with me, for I am poor and hungry.'

'A small boon indeed,' said Gwawl, and he ordered his servants to fill the sack. But however much bread and meat they put into it, it was no fuller than when they started.

'Will your bag never be full?' asked Gwawl, amazed.

'It will not,' said Pwyll, as Rhiannon had told him to say, 'until a man who possesses wide lands and great riches treads down with both his feet the food which is in the bag and says: "Enough has been put in here."'

'Go quickly, lord,' said Rhiannon to Gwawl, 'and tread down the food into the bag, otherwise there will be no meat left in my father's house.'

'I shall indeed do so,' said Gwawl, and he rose and put both feet into the sack. But before he could say, 'Enough has been put in here,' Pwyll had closed the sides of the sack over his head and fastened it with a thong. Then he blew his horn and immediately his men came in from the orchard where they had been waiting. Gwawl's followers, taken by surprise, were easily overpowered and locked away, and Pwyll threw off his ragged clothes and took his place at Rhiannon's side.

And as each one of his men came by the sack on his way to sit at the feasting, he asked, 'What is in here?'

'A badger,' he was answered, and so he struck at the sack: and thus was the game of Badger in the Bag played for the first time.

But at last Gwawl cried out from within the sack, 'Have mercy on me, for I am too great a man to be killed in a sack.'

'He speaks truly,' said Heveydd Hen to Pwyll. 'He deserves a better fate.'

'Let him give an oath never to seek vengeance for what has been done to him today, and let him go free,' said Rhiannon.

'Willingly shall I do as Heveydd Hen and Rhiannon counsel me,' said Pwyll.

When Gwawl had sworn to take no vengeance for what had been done to him, he was freed from the sack and he returned to his own lands, and all his followers with him. But Pwyll and the men of Dyved feasted long into the night in the house of Heveydd Hen in celebration of the marriage of Rhiannon. And the next day Pwyll set out with Rhiannon for his own land of Dyved.

When four years were passed, a son was born to Rhiannon and Pwyll and there was great rejoicing at Narberth. But that same night, as Rhiannon lay sleeping with the child in the cradle close by, the six women who were in the room to watch over them fell asleep, and when they awoke the child was gone. They searched everywhere but could not find him, and they were in great terror.

'We shall be put to death for this,' they said. 'There is no hope for us.' And in their terror, to save themselves, they killed a hound pup and smeared its blood on Rhiannon and laid its bones beside her. When she awoke in the morning and asked for her son, they said, 'Lady, why do·you ask for the child? In the night you killed and devoured him, in spite of our struggles to save him.'

'That cannot be,' said Rhiannon. 'Where is my child? Tell me the truth, I beg you, and I will see that you come to no harm.' But they held to their tale, in spite of her pleading.

For all Pwyll might try to hide it, the tale of the terrible thing that Rhiannon had done to her child spread throughout all Dyved, and Pwyll's lords came to him and counselled him to put away Rhiannon and take another wife. But Pwyll loved her, and he would not do as they asked. 'Let her be punished,' he said, 'but I will not set her aside.'

So it was decreed that for seven years Rhiannon should sit every day at the gate of the castle of Narberth, and to every stranger that approached she should tell the tale of her crime and offer to carry him on her back into the courtyard. But, for pity of her, there were few of those to whom she told her story who would permit this. And so the days passed.

Now, at that time there was a good man named Teirnyon in Gwent Is Coed, and he owned a fine mare, the finest in the land. Every year, on the night of the first of May, this mare gave birth to a foal. Yet always, before morning, the foal was gone. But when the first of May came round in that year when Pwyll's son was born, Teirnyon said to his wife, 'Come what may, tonight I shall watch in the stable and see what happens to the foal.'

So he sat up all night near the mare, and she gave birth to a fine colt. Suddenly Teirnyon heard a great noise from outside and a long arm with a huge clawed hand came in through the window and seized the colt by the mane. Teirnyon drew his sword and cut off the arm by the elbow so that it fell in through the window. Immediately there was a great wailing and howling from outside. Teirnyon rushed from the stable, but he could see nothing in the darkness; and when the wailing had died away, he returned to the mare and her colt, and there in the doorway of the stable he saw a young babe wrapped in rich swaddling clothes. He took the child to his wife, and they brought him up as their own son.

The boy grew fast and was soon as tall and strong as a child of twice his age. When he was four years old, Teirnyon gave him for his own the colt which had been born on the night he had been found. And in that same year, tidings reached Gwent Is Coed of Rhiannon and her crime and the punishment she suffered. Teirnyon looked closely at the boy and saw his likeness to Pwyll, whom he had once served, in years past. 'Lady,' he said to his wife, 'this is Pwyll's son. It is not right that we should keep him from his father. Nor is it just that Rhiannon should suffer longer for an offence of which she is innocent.'

'We must send him to his own home,' agreed Teirnyon's wife, though she was sad to lose him.

So the very next day Teirnyon set out for Narberth and the boy went with him, riding on the horse which Teirnyon had given to him. As they approached the castle, Rhiannon came to meet them and offered to carry them into the court-yard. 'For this is my punishment for slaying and devouring my own son,' she said.

'Lady,' said Teirnyon, 'I would not consider allowing such a thing.'

'Nor I,' said the boy.

They went on into the castle where Pwyll greeted Teirnyon gladly and made him welcome, and they sat down to eat. And Pwyll set Teirnyon in the honoured place, between him and Rhiannon. While they ate, Teirnyon said, 'I have a strange story to tell you, lord,' and he told them of the mare and the long arm and the boy he had found, four years before. 'Look at him,' said Tiernyon. 's there anyone who can deny that he is the son of Pwyll?' He turned to Rhiannon.

'It is your child, lady, who was stolen from you on the night he was born, and those who told that tale of you, they lied.'

There was, indeed, no one there, who, looking at the child, did not believe he was Pwyll's son, the likeness was so strong; and there was great rejoicing throughout Dyved when the truth was known. The boy was named Pryderi, and he grew up to be the fairest youth, and the best skilled at games, of all in his father's kingdom. And when, in time, Pwyll died, Pryderi ruled after him, and was much loved by all.

*

Pwyll, here a Welsh prince, was originally a god of the under-world; and his wife, Rhiannon, a goddess, possibly of the sky or the moon. Rhiannon survives in one legendary form or another until we meet her again in the story of King Arthur, as the mysterious Lady of the Lake. The names by which the Lady of the Lake was known – Nimue and Vivien – arose, it has been suggested, as the result of a series of miscopyings of the name Rhiannon, made by successive scribes throughout the Middle Ages. This seems very possible, since names, which often have in themselves no apparent or obvious mean-ing, are the most difficult of all words to transcribe from a poor hand or a badly written manuscript.

Gwawl means 'light', so Rhiannon's rejected suitor was probably, in the first instance, a sun god; if so, in its earliest form, the story of the marriage of Pwyll and Rhiannon and the game of Badger in the Bag, must have been a myth of the temporary and ever-repeated victory of night and darkness over day.

Bran, Son of Llyr

WHEN the world was younger than it is today, there ruled in Britain a tall and mighty king, so huge that no house was large enough for him, Bran, the son of Llyr. He had a brother, Manawyddan, and a sister, Branwen, and two half-brothers, Nissyen and Evnissyen, the sons of his mother. Of these two young men, Nissyen was gentle and peaceable, but Evnissyen was turbulent and delighted in all manner of strife and would often try to set his brothers quarrelling among themselves for the pleasure that it gave to him.

One time, when Bran was keeping his court at Harlech, there came to him over the sea from Ireland Matholwch, the king of that land, to woo fair Branwen. It pleased Bran that there should be friendship between Britain and Ireland and he willingly gave his sister to Matholwch. A great wedding feast was held for them, and they ate and drank and talked together in great goodwill, the men of Britain with the men of Ireland.

But while the feasting was yet unfinished, Evnissyen, who had been journeying, returned to court, and as he rode into the castle he saw how the stables were filled with strange horses. 'Whose are those horses?' he asked.

'They are the horses of Matholwch, king of Ireland, he who has married Branwen,' he was told.

Immediately Evnissyen flew into a rage. 'The fairest maiden in the world, and my sister. And they have given her to this Matholwch without my consent.' And in his spite and anger he cut off the ears and the tails of all the king of Ireland's horses and so disfigured and mutilated them that they were useless.

When word was brought to Matholwch of what had been done to his horses, he was amazed. 'It is an intended insult to you, lord, and you must not bear it,' his followers told him.

But Matholwch said, 'Bran and his brothers have received me kindly and given me their sister for my wife. Why should they now insult me? There is some misunderstanding.'

Yet his men entreated him and reminded him of the pride which should be a king's and said, 'You can remain no longer in a place where you have been so flouted, lord. You must go from here this very day.' So that finally Matholwch was persuaded by their repeated demands, and made ready to go.

When Bran heard that Matholwch was preparing to return to Ireland without taking leave of him, he sent two of his men to ask why he acted thus. Matholwch said, 'I have been dishonoured and insulted,' and he told them of his horses.

'Indeed, lord,' said the messengers, 'it was not by the will of Bran that this thing was done, and the dishonour of it is greater for him than for you.'

'Truly,' said Matholwch bitterly, 'that is as I think also. Yet the insult cannot be recalled.'

Bran was greatly distressed at the thought that Matholwch would leave Britain with ill feelings in his heart towards him, and he said, 'There is nothing that I would not do to prevent bloodshed between our two lands. Go to Matholwch and tell him that had any other man than my brother done this thing to him against my will, he should die for it, but the son of my mother I cannot kill. Yet say to Matholwch that for every horse that he has lost, I shall give him another. And I shall give to him, besides, a staff of silver as tall as himself, and a plate of gold.'

Matholwch's counsellors advised him to accept Bran's offer,

and so make sure of redress. Accordingly he returned with all his men to Bran's court and they feasted and made merry once more. But Matholwch laughed and smiled less than he had formerly, and seeing this, Bran was grieved and said, 'If it is because I have not given you enough in satisfaction for my brother's insult, that you are sad tonight, I will give to you as well my cauldron, which will make dead men live again. If one of your warriors should die, you have only to cast his body into the cauldron and he will live again and be even as he was before, save that he will have lost the power of speech.'

Matholwch was gladdened by this most profitable gift, and when the time came, he parted from Bran in great friendship and set sail for Ireland in thirteen ships, taking Branwen and the cauldron with him. Yet his kinsmen and those closest about him were not satisfied and they still murmured amongst themselves against Bran and his brothers.

For a year Matholwch dwelt in happiness with Branwen and a son was born to them whom they named Gwern. But soon after this Matholwch's kinsmen and counsellors began to speak openly against Branwen, because of the insult Evnissyen had put on their king, and they blamed Matholwch for parting from Bran in peace, and they urged him to avenge insult by insult and put away the queen. And at last, to end their demands, Matholwch sent Branwen from his side and set her to work in the kitchen of his castle. And there in the kitchen she toiled for three years, ill-treated and mocked at by the scullions.

But Branwen tamed a starling and taught it to speak, telling it of her brother Bran and how to find him; and at the end of the three years she wrote a letter telling of her sorrows and the insult that was done to her, tied it beneath the starling's wing, and released the bird to fly to Britain. The starling flew towards Britain, and there it sought out Bran and alighted on his shoulder to perch there, fluttering its wings so that Bran might see the letter. When Bran knew of all his sister suffered, he was angry and gathered together a great army, then, leaving his young son Caradawc to rule in Britain, he set off for Ireland with all his ships. Yet there was no ship large enough for Bran himself, so he had to wade across the sea to Ireland.

One morning Matholwch's swineherds, who had been keeping his pigs along the shore, close by the sea, came hurrying to him. 'Lord,' they said, 'we have seen a strange thing today: a wood growing on the sea, and beside the wood a mountain which moved, and on top of the mountain a high ridge with a lake on either side of it, coming from the land of Britain. What can this mean, lord?'

'I do not know,' replied Matholwch. 'But if it comes from Britain, then maybe Branwen knows. Ask her what it means.'

So the swineherds went to the kitchen and told Branwen of what they had seen, asking her its meaning. Branwen smiled. 'It is the men of Britain, coming to avenge my wrongs. That forest which you saw, it is the masts of their ships, and that mountain is Bran, my brother. The high ridge on the mountain is his nose, and the two lakes are his two eyes, and he is angry for my sake as he looks towards Ireland.'

The men of Ireland were afraid and they broke down the bridge across the river that lay between them and the coast, and took counsel together as to how best they should meet Bran. Meanwhile, Bran and the men of Britain landed on the shore of Ireland and marched inland until they came to the river, and there they found no bridge to cross it by. 'Lord,' said his men to Bran, 'how shall we cross?'

'The man who would be a leader,' said Bran, 'let him be a bridge.' And he lay down over the river, from bank to bank, and the army marched across him. And even as the last man stepped on to the farther bank and Bran rose to his feet again, they saw the counsellors of Matholwch coming to meet them with an offer. 'Your sister's son, Gwern, shall be king of Ireland if it pleases you,' they said. 'Matholwch will give up the kingdom to him.'

'Having had the toil and trouble of coming to Ireland,' said Bran, 'am I then not to have Matholwch's kingdom for myself?'

Matholwch's men went back to him and told him of Bran's answer. 'My friends,' he said, 'tell me what I should do.'

The men of Ireland considered their plight and then they said to their king, 'Lord, Bran has never yet lived in a house, for no house is large enough for him. Build him a house that he can live in, and he may perhaps make peace with you.'

Bran accepted this offer, and the men of Ireland built him a house with a hundred pillars to support its roof, and large enough for even him to live in. But Matholwch's counsellors were crafty, and when the house was ready, they secretly set hooks on either side of the hundred pillars, and on each hook they hung a leather sack, and in each sack there was hidden an armed man. Then they sent word to Bran to come into his house.

But Evnissyen elbowed aside his brothers and strode forward and came first into the house, frowning and looking about him. When he saw the sack hanging from the nearest pillar, he pointed to one of them and asked, 'What is in that sack?'

'Flour, my friend,' said one of Matholwch's men.

Evnissyen felt the sack with his hands, and he felt the man through the leather; so he moved his hands about until he found the man's head and crushed it between his fingers. Then he turned to the second sack. 'What is in this sack?'

'Flour, my friend,' he was told again.

With the man in that sack Evnissyen did as he had done with the other; and so with them all, until by the time when Bran entered his house with his followers, and with him Matholwch and his lords, there was not an armed man left alive in any of the sacks.

The men of Britain and the men of Ireland and Branwen with them sat down together peaceably and the kingdom was bestowed on Gwern. When all had been concluded in friendship, Bran called the boy to him and kissed him and made much of him, and Manawyddan and Nissyen did likewise; and the boy smiled at them and kissed his three uncles each in turn.

But Evnissyen frowned and said, 'Am I not also his uncle? Why does the boy not come to me?'

'Go to him, nephew,' said Bran.

Gwern smiled and went to Evnissyen, who rose and caught hold of him, and before any there guessed what he would do, he threw him into the huge fire that blazed upon the hearth. Branwen cried out in horror and would have run into the fire in a vain attempt to save her son, but Bran held her back. Then everyone there, the men of Britain and the men of Ireland alike, seized their weapons, streaming out from the new house to the plain beyond and falling upon each other.

Great was the slaughter amongst them, and for many days did they fight; but always the men of Ireland had the advantage, for no matter how many of them were killed, at the end of the day's fighting their comrades would carry them to the cauldron which Bran had given to Matholwch and cast them into it, and in the morning they would step out from the cauldron, alive and well, save that they could no longer speak.

When Evnissyen saw this, and saw also how those men of Britain who had died stayed dead, he was grieved. 'I have been the cause of this great sorrow,' he said. 'I will now undo my deed.' Stripping off his arms that he might not be known,

he lay down amongst the bodies of the Irish. When Matholwch's warriors came to gather up their slain comrades, they
took up Evnissyen with them and flung him into the cauldron. In the cauldron, with all his strength, he stretched
himself out, so that the cauldron was broken into four pieces,
and his heart burst also.

After that, those men of Ireland who were killed in battle
stayed dead, so that in the end the victory went to the men
of Britain, for all the Irish were slain. But it was a fruitless
victory, for of all the men of Britain who had come to Ireland,
only eight remained alive, among them Bran and his brother
Manawyddan, Pryderi, son of Pwyll, and Taliesin the bard.
But Bran was sorely wounded and knew he could not live, so
he commanded his seven friends to cut off his head. 'Take my
head and return to Britain,' he said. 'Carry it to London and
bury it on the White Mount, with the face towards France.
So long as it remains buried there no enemy shall invade
Britain from over the sea. Yet you may take many years in
your journey to London. In Harlech you shall feast for seven
years, while the birds of Rhiannon sing to you; and on the
isle of Gwales, off Pembrokeshire, you will remain for fourscore years. And in all those years you shall be happy, with
your sorrows forgotten, and my head shall talk and laugh
with you, even as I have done in my lifetime. But when, in
Gwales, you open a door which faces towards Cornwall, then
you will remember your grief; and then you must go on to
London, and bury my head.'

They did as their king commanded them, and cut off Bran's
head and sailed for Britain. And Branwen went with them.
When they came to Britain they found that Bran's son, Caradawc, was dead, and a stranger had been crowned king in
London.

Branwen wept and looked back towards Ireland. 'It would
have been better had I never been born,' she said. 'Through

me two lands have been destroyed.' Then her heart broke and
she died.

But the others went on to Harlech, bearing Bran's head
with them, and at Harlech they stopped to rest. There the
three birds of Rhiannon came to them, singing songs so sweet
that all other songs seemed to them hateful in comparison.
In Harlech they remained feasting for seven years, even as
Bran had foretold, then they went on to Gwales – which is
now called Grassholm – and found there a fine house awaiting
them, with three doors. Two of the doors were open, but one
– that which faced towards Cornwall – was closed. 'That,'
said Manawyddan, 'is the door we may not open.' And they
all kept from it.

On Gwales they remained feasting for fourscore years,
their sorrows utterly forgotten, and Bran's head spoke with
them as he had done in life, so that they were happy.

But one day, when fourscore years were passed, one of
them said, 'Why should I not open the door to find out
whether it was true or not, what Bran foretold of it?' And he
opened the door and looked out towards Cornwall. Immediately the seven companions remembered all their sorrows and
grief – the loss of their friends and the death of Bran – and a
great unrest came upon them, so that they were compelled
to journey on towards London. And there, in London, on the
White Mount, they buried Bran's head.

Yet it is said that, years later, King Arthur dug it up, for,
he declared, it was right that the land of Britain should owe
its freedom to the courage of its living men, and not to the
magical powers of a dead king's head.

*

*The White Mount, in London, is probably the spot where
now the Tower of London stands.*

Manawyddan, the last surviving child of Llyr, married the

widowed Rhiannon, mother of Pryderi. The magical birds of Rhiannon were said to be able to sing the dead to life and the living into a sleep of death. They sang but seldom, however, as an old Welsh saying tells us: There are three things which are not often heard: the singing of the birds of Rhiannon, wise words from the mouth of an Englishman, and an invitation to a feast from a miser.

Taliesin

The Welsh poet Taliesin really lived, probably in the sixth
century A.D., possibly at about the same time as the historical Arthur, and there are extant a number of poems ascribed
to him. It is unlikely that he wrote all of them, but certain of
them are no doubt his.

In the following tale he is shown not only as a poet, but
as a magician and a prophet, also. The story is the least old
of the three in this Welsh section — the earliest surviving
manuscript of it being as late as the end of the sixteenth
century — but the poems quoted in it are much older. It is
possible that the story of Elphin ap Gwyddno and his troubles
was composed during the Middle Ages to provide a connect-
ing link for a number of old Welsh poems — not necessarily
by the real Taliesin. Yet, sophisticated and modern though
this tale may be in comparison with the two which precede
it, it has echoes of the very early past. The witch Ceridwen is
an ancient British goddess who was possibly the patroness of
poetic inspiration; and the theme of the pursuer and his
quarry changing shape during the pursuit, is old indeed.

The young Taliesin may remind us, in his precociousness,
of that other youthful wonder-worker, the enchanter Merlin,
when he explained the riddle of King Vortigern's fallen
walls; while Elphin's masterly deductions from the severed
finger should surely win him a respected place amongst the
amateur detectives of literature.

THERE lived in Penllyn, a great while ago, an enchantress named Ceridwen, who had a son who was the ugliest lad ever seen. Now, Ceridwen thought that, by reason of his ugliness, it might be hard indeed for her son to make his way in the world, and she determined to brew for him a draught of wisdom and understanding; so that if men could not admire him for his looks, they would be forced to respect him for his knowledge of everything that had been in the past and all that would be in the future. Therefore, to this end she gathered together, at the right season of the day or night, all the charm-bearing herbs she needed, threw them into a huge cauldron and set it to boil over a fire for a year and a day. Then, because she could not both tend the cauldron and gather more herbs at one and the same time, she set a blind man named Morda to feed the fire with sticks and keep the flames well fanned, and a boy named Gwion to stir the broth.

For almost a year things went well; and then one morning when Ceridwen was out in the woods and fields picking herbs and speaking her spells over them, Gwion chanced to stir the cauldron too carelessly, and three drops of the boiling liquid splashed on to his hand. To ease the pain of the scalding, Gwion licked his hand with his tongue, and instantly he knew all that had passed and all that was to come; and the very first thing of all others that seemed to him important, was that once the year and the day were over and the boiling was done, Ceridwen meant no good to him. So straightway he dropped the ladle into the cauldron and fled from the house.

As soon as he had gone, with no one to watch the cauldron, the liquid boiled over and the cauldron burst and the draught of wisdom and understanding was lost. When Ceridwen returned and saw what had happened, in her anger she snatched up a stick of firewood and struck Morda with it.

'I am not to blame,' he cried out. 'It was the boy Gwion.'

Ceridwen looked about her and saw that Gwion had gone. 'You speak truly,' she said. 'It was indeed Gwion.' And she ran out of the house and after him.

When Gwion looked back over his shoulder and saw her coming – and gaining on him, too – with his new-found understanding he turned himself into a hare and made better speed. But Ceridwen changed herself into a greyhound and caught up with him on the bank of a river. Barely in time he changed himself into a fish and leapt into the stream and swam thankfully away beneath the water. But Ceridwen changed herself into an otter and swam in pursuit of the fish. With the otter's jaws almost closing on him, Gwion became a bird and flew high into the air. But in the form of a hawk, Ceridwen flew above him and swooped. Yet before her talons could grasp him, he espied below a heap of wheat lying just within the doorway of a barn. He dropped down upon it and became a grain of wheat amongst all the others. Immediately Ceridwen changed herself into a black hen which scratched and pecked in the wheat until she found the one grain that was Gwion and she swallowed it. Then she took once again her own shape, believing that she was rid of him.

Yet she was mistaken, for in due course of time she gave birth to a child, and this child was Gwion. But the child was so beautiful that even Ceridwen had not the heart to kill him, so instead she tied him in a leathern bag and threw him into the sea: and this was on the twenty-ninth day of April.

At that time a lord named Gwyddno ruled in those parts, and he had a salmon-weir near Aberystwyth, close by his castle. Each year the salmon would come up from the sea to the rivers and streams to spawn, and it was Gwyddno's custom each May eve to give the right to net his weir to a friend or follower whom he wished to favour. And the gift was not little one, for the worth of the salmon netted in Gwyddno's weir each May eve was one hundred pieces of gold.

Now, Gwyddno had an only son, a youth named Elphin, who was – save in the matter of his young wife, who was good and kind – the unluckiest man in all Wales, with never a penny to bless himself with and ill fortune coming to all he undertook. That year, in the hope that thereby he might at least gain a hundred gold pieces worth of fish, Gwyddno gave his son the right to net the weir.

Accordingly, on May eve Elphin arose and went to the weir eagerly, hoping his luck might turn. Yet that year, for the very first time since men could remember, there was not a single salmon in the weir, but only a leathern bag, carried up from the sea and caught fast against a pole.

'Truly,' said the weir-keeper, 'you bring ill luck wherever you go, Elphin ap Gwyddno. For all the years that I have dwelt here, the salmon have been thisk in this weir upon May eve. Today you come, and what have we but an old leathern bag and nothing else.'

Elphin, trying hard to hide his disappointment, attempted a jest. 'Who knows, there might be a hundred gold pieces in that bag. Draw it in and let us open it.'

There were murmurs and jeers as the dripping bag was hooked out of the water and handed to Elphin; and everyone there gathered round to see what might be inside, ready to laugh. But when they saw the child, they exclaimed at his beauty. 'Behold a radiant brow!' said one of them, and Elphin, looking at the boy in wonder, said, 'A radiant brow indeed. Let him be called Taliesin.' And so he was, from that day on, since that is the meaning of the name.

Elphin laid the child in the bag carefully on his horse, and mounting, rode home at an easy pace so that the child should journey in comfort. Yet he could not help but feel sorry that his ill luck had held and that he had not a single salmon to

carry back with him. Then, suddenly, from the bag, Taliesin made a poem for Elphin, to cheer him, and it was the first song that he ever made.

> Fair Elphin, cease from complaining,
> No man need be discontented with his lot;
> Despair never brought any gaining,
> And none may foretell his fate . . .
>
> Weep not : never from Gwyddno's weir
> Came there better luck than today.
> Good never flows from despair.
> Though I be small, my gifts are great. . . .
>
> Little I may be and weak;
> Yet when the day of your needing comes,
> Of more worth I'll prove than the salmon you seek.
> Fair Elphin, mourn not your fate. . . .

When Elphin reached his father's castle, Gwyddno said, 'Had you a good haul at the weir, my son?'

'I had a good haul from the weir, father,' replied Elphin cheerfully. 'I had something better than fish.'

'And what was that?'

Elphin took the child out of the bag and held him up. 'A poet, father.'

Gwyddno exclaimed in dismay, 'What will a poet profit you, my son?'

It was Taliesin who answered him, clearly and boldly. 'A poet will profit him more than the weir ever profited you.'

Gwyddno was astonished. 'Can you speak, and you so little?'

'I can speak better than you can question me,' replied Taliesin, and forthwith he made a poem, telling them of his skill and his power of foreknowledge, so that everyone who heard him marvelled.

Elphin gave the child to his wife, and for thirteen years they cared for him with love and kindness; and in all that time Elphin had good luck at last. His crops and his cattle prospered and he grew rich, and was as much respected as he had been slighted before.

When Taliesin was thirteen years old, Elphin was bidden by his uncle, Maelgwn Gwynedd, the king, to spend the Christmastide feasting at his court. Elphin set off for the king's castle, taking Taliesin with him.

At court, during the feasting, in the presence of Maelgwn and his queen, the talk turned to flattery, and the courtiers and the vassals all vied with one another in praising the king's possessions. 'Is there anywhere in all the world a king so great as Maelgwn?' they asked. 'Has anyone a lovelier, a wiser and more virtuous queen? Has anyone poets more skilled? Horses swifter? Hounds more eager in the chase?' And so it went on, with all Maelgwn's possessions being acclaimed the best in the world, and none of them receiving more praise than his wife and his four and twenty poets.

And when there was nothing else left to flatter, and everyone was silent and the king was sitting, smiling and well pleased, on his throne, Elphin, simple and loyal, said into the silence, 'Only a king may vie with a king. But were Maelgwn Gwynedd not a king, I would say that my wife was better than his, and my poet more skilled.'

King Maelgwn was furious and, for daring to speak as he had, he caused Elphin to be imprisoned in a dark tower with chains about his wrists and ankles. It is said that the chains were of silver, because Elphin was of royal blood; but that will not have made them – nor will it have made Elphin's heart – any the lighter.

As soon as the Christmas feasting was over, the king sent his son, Rhun, to Elphin's castle to test the truth of Elphin's boast. Rhun was an unpleasing young man, ever ready to cause trouble and mischief, and he left his father's court determined to bring disgrace on Elphin's wife. But Taliesin left the court before him, and riding hard, reached home in time to warn her. She was greatly distressed to hear of the misfortune that had befallen Elphin, but Taliesin reassured her saying, 'If you will but do as I say, then all will come well in the end.' And he bade her change clothes with one of her kitchen wenches, put the girl in her own apartments and set her in her own place at table. This Elphin's wife made haste to do, arraying the girl in her best gown and decking her with her jewels, even giving to her Elphin's signet ring which he had left with her.

When Rhun arrived at the castle that evening, he was greeted by the kitchen wench in her mistress's garments, made welcome and bidden to sit down and sup with her. All during the meal Rhun laughed and jested with the woman whom he supposed to be Elphin's wife. Time after time he refilled her cup with strong wine. The kitchen wench, giggling and babbling, became more and more drunk, until at last she fell asleep across the table. Rhun took a knife and cut off her little finger on which she was wearing Elphin's ring, and so drunk and so heavily asleep was she, that she felt nothing of it. Then Rhun and his friends went from the castle and rode back to court.

King Maelgwn was well satisfied at the way things had gone and he had Elphin brought from his prison. 'I have proved you a liar, my nephew,' he said. 'In vain you boasted of your wife and declared her virtues to be above the virtues of my queen. See, here is your wife's finger, with your ring upon it, cut from her hand yesterday, while she lay in a drunken sleep.' Smiling complacently, he ordered one of his squires to give the finger to Elphin, who received it with horror.

Standing before the king in his silver chains, Elphin examined the finger closely, then with a sigh of relief he looked up and smiled. 'I cannot deny that this is indeed my ring, but this is not my wife's finger, and I can give you three good reasons why it is not. The first is this: this is the little finger from a hand, and the ring fits tightly upon it – but my wife can hardly keep my ring from slipping off her thumb. The second reason is that since I have known my wife, she has never missed paring her nails on a Saturday, before going to bed. The nail on this finger has not been cut for a month. And this is the third reason: the hand from which this finger came had been kneading dough not three days before – there is hardened dough about the nail – and I know that my wife has not kneaded dough since she married me. So you see, lord uncle, though it is my ring, it is not my wife's finger.'

The king was very angry, but he did not see what more he could say in the matter, without having Elphin's wife brought before him, that he might count the number of her fingers; so he said, 'Nevertheless, you have still to make good your boast in the matter of your poet.' And he had Elphin taken back to the tower. And there Elphin, in his silver chains, lay wondering whether he would ever be freed.

In Elphin's home, too, when she heard that he had been thrown once more into prison, his wife wondered if she would ever see her husband again; but Taliesin said to her confidently, 'Be glad and rejoice, lady, for I shall go to court and free my master.'

'How can you, a mere boy, set him free?' she asked; and he answered her in a poem:

> 'A journey I shall make,
> The king's gate I shall reach,
> The king's hall I shall enter in,
> And there shall sing my song.
> I shall speak my speech
> To silence the king's bards,

To greet them all with mockery
And set them all at naught
Before their leader's eyes.
Thus Elphin I shall free.'

Then Taliesin set off for the court of King Maelgwn to free Elphin. At the king's castle he slipped quietly into the great hall and sat down in a corner, near where the poets stood when they entertained the king while he ate and drank. When the time came, and the king was seated at his meal, his poets – all four and twenty of them, led by his chief bard Heinin – filed with great pomp and dignity up the hall to sing and chant the praises of their master. On their way they passed by the dark corner where Taliesin sat, and as they passed him, he pouted out his lips at them, and flicking a finger up and down against his lips, he made a foolish noise.

The poets stood before King Maelgwn and bowed low to him, then they made ready to sing, but not a word could they utter, and all they could do was to pout out their lips at him and flick their fingers against their lips and make a foolish noise.

Maelgwn was astonished. Then, supposing them to be drunk, he sent one of his nobles to them, to remind them of where they were, and to bid them cease their foolishness and sing and recite with no more delay. But they paid no heed to the message. A second time the king sent to them, again with no success. Then Maelgwn grew annoyed. 'Bid them leave the hall,' he said. 'I am better off without such fools.'

Yet the poets did not move from where they stood, and only went on making the foolish noise with their fingers and their pouted lips. At that the king became more angry and bade one of his squires strike Heinin, to bring him to his senses.

The squire took up a stick and struck Heinin over the head, and at that Heinin became himself once more, and all the other poets with him. Heinin was aghast and fell upon his knees. 'Most honoured king, forgive us, for we were under a spell, so that we could neither speak nor sing. And I warrant that the spell was laid on us by that spirit that sits in the corner there, in the form of a child.'

'Fetch me that child or spirit,' demanded the king; and his squire brought Taliesin to him. 'Who are you and from where do you come?' asked Maelgwn, who had not noticed Taliesin amongst Elphin's followers at Christmastide.

Taliesin answered in verse:

> 'Chief bard I am to Elphin;
>   My first home was the land of the summer stars;
>   In time all kings shall call me Taliesin.'

He went on to speak of all the ages he had lived and all the happenings he had witnessed, ending:

> 'I was born of the witch Ceridwen;
>   Once I was little Gwion,
>   Who now am Taliesin.'

The king and all his court heard him with wonder, for never had they listened to such a poem from one so young. But the king was angry because Taliesin was Elphin's poet, and in spite of his admiration for the boy, he did not want his own poets to be surpassed by Elphin's. So he bade Heinin and his other poets answer Taliesin in verse and vie with him: but all they could do was once again to pout out their lips and make a foolish noise with their fingers.

From beneath lowered brows the king looked sullenly at Taliesin. 'Why have you come here?' he demanded.

Again Taliesin answered him in a long poem, declaring that he had come to free his master Elphin, and threatening the king should he not release him. Yet still Maelgwn sat angry and sullen, and Taliesin with his singing called up a storm, his words filling the hall with sound and echoing through the rafters.

> 'Guess what it is:
> Created before the Flood;
> Strong and mighty,
> Without bones or blood;
> Without flesh, without veins,
> No head and no feet;
> Without needs or fears;
> No older it grows
> With the passing years.
> At its coming the sea grows white;
> Without feet it walks through the wood;
> Without hands passes over the field.
> Though as old as the oldest,
> To old age it does not yield.
> As wide it is
> As the whole wide earth.
> It has never been seen,
> And it had no birth.
> It goes where it will
> On sea or on land;
> It may not be prisoned;
> It comes not at command.
> No equal it has;
> Noisy, discourteous, bad –
> One moment here;
> Silent, good and gentle –
> The next moment there.
> It will bring destruction,
> And never repair the wrong.
> It can be blamed for no actions;
> It is weak, it is strong;
> It is wet, it is dry;
> It is late, it is soon;

From the heat of the sun it arises,
From the cold of the moon. . . .

And now with its mighty breath
It comes to bring vengeance and death
Upon Maelgwn Gwynedd.'

By the time that Taliesin had ended his song, it was the storm, not his words, which was filling the hall with sound; so that hangings were blown down from the walls, sparks were scattered from the fires and the torches were put out; and it was the wind, not his voice, that was echoing through the rafters and howling round the heads of the king and his court.

'Fetch Elphin from the tower,' shouted Maelgwn above the uproar, and someone ran to do his bidding.

When Elphin had been brought, the wind hushed and the storm died down, and Taliesin spoke a verse and Elphin's silver chains fell about his feet and he was free once more.

Then Taliesin made several poems to prove he was more skilled than Heinin or any of Maelgwn's poets; so that even Maelgwn was forced to admit it. And when Taliesin had sent for Elphin's wife, and shown to the king and to Rhun, his son, and to all the others there, that she had no finger missing from her hands, the king made peace with Elphin, and, thankful that his castle still stood, he ordered a great feasting and merrymaking, and everyone sat down to eat and drink in friendship.

Then, while the wine was being drunk, and men were growing boastful, Taliesin whispered to Elphin to wager the king that his horse was fleeter than any in the royal stables. The king took up the challenge; and on the very next morning he chose a course for the racing and sent for four and twenty of his best steeds, to be matched against Elphin's horse.

While the horses were being made ready for the race, Taliesin went to the youth who was to ride Elphin's horse and gave him four and twenty little twigs of holly. 'At the outset of the contest, let all the king's horses pass you,' he said, 'and then overtake them, one by one. As you come up with each one, strike it with one of these twigs, and thus shall you win the race for our master.' This the youth willingly agreed to do. 'Yet one thing more,' said Taliesin. 'Mark well the place where our master's horse shall stumble while it gallops.' This, also, the youth promised to do.

Because of Taliesin's enchantments, Elphin's horse won the race; and at that place where it stumbled while galloping, the rider threw down his cap; and there, afterwards, Taliesin bade Elphin dig. Surprised, Elphin set men to dig, and in that very spot, deep in the ground, they found a large cauldron filled with gold.

'It is a reward to you and to your wife, good master,' said Taliesin to Elphin, 'for having taken me out of the weir, and for all your years of kindness to me.'

After that, Taliesin achieved great fame throughout all Wales, both for his poems and for his prophecies, and was reckoned the best poet of all.

SCOTLAND

Finn MacCool

Finn Mac Cool – or Fingal, as he is sometimes known – is the great hero of the Gaelic-speaking peoples, as much loved in Scotland and the Isle of Man as in Ireland. Though the scene of his exploits is mainly Ireland, there are place-names connected with him and his companions all over the West Highlands. On the shoulder of Ben Eadden, in Argyllshire, there is a flight of rocky steps which are known as Fingal's Stair; on Skye, in Kilmuir, there is a rock formation like a wall, running up an almost perpendicular incline, called the Wall of the Fianna and, at the head of Portree Loch, there is a mountain known as Fingal's Seat. And on Staffa there is the famous Fingal's Cave which inspired Mendelssohn's overture.

Finn and his men of the Fianna are popularly supposed to have lived in the third century A.D. The early historical writers of Ireland believed the Fianna to have been a standing army maintained by the High Kings as a defence against the raids of the Norsemen, and Finn to have been at one time its general. However, these two traditions cannot be reconciled, as there were no Viking attacks on Ireland as early as the third century. Many of the stories about Finn and his men are certainly concerned with their enmity with the men of Lochlann, that is, the Norsemen – Lochlann being an ancient name for one of the Scandinavian countries, probably Norway – but this is no doubt because the tales, already old at the time of the Viking raids in the eighth, ninth and

*tenth centuries, will have been retold then by storytellers
who substituted the very real menace of a contemporary foe
for the original adversaries of the heroes.*

*Many of the stories told about Finn and the Fianna have
their roots in myths far older than the third century, and
other stories, far later than the third century, have since
been gathered round his name. For hundreds of years Finn
Mac Cool has provided an example of courage, daring and
honour; and the old tales about him and his comrades are
still told and loved in the Highlands and the Isles of Scotland.*

*Scottish and Irish traditions about Finn vary, but usually
only in detail. In the following account of Finn, I have kept
largely to Scottish sources.*

IN the very old days, when both Scotland and Ireland were
harried by the Norsemen, there was in Ireland a band of
hardy warriors, the Fianna, whose task it was to drive away
the raiders from their shores and to fight, when need be, for
the High King who ruled at Tara.

Now, at that time when Conn of the Hundred Battles
was High King of Ireland, the leader of the Fianna was Cool,
chief of the Clan Baskin. But Cool quarrelled with the chief
of another clan, Gaul Mac Morna, head of the Clan Morna,
who was jealous of his leadership. The Clan Baskin and the
Clan Morna, under their two chiefs, fought a battle, and in
the fighting Cool was slain by Gaul, who thereby became
leader of the Fianna. Cool's followers went into exile and his
wife fled to a place of safety. A few months after Cool's
death, she gave birth to his son.

A sister of Cool, named Fleet Foot from the speed at which
she could run, took the child to a wild place in the woods,
where no man from the Clan Morna was likely to find him.
There she made a house in a tree where they lived in safety.

Cool's son grew into a fine, strong boy with yellow hair, and from Fleet Foot he learnt all manner of feats of strength, running and swimming and leaping. It is said that she taught him to swim by throwing him into the water again and again, until he could at last swim over nine waves faster than she herself could swim. She taught him to leap by digging a pit in the ground and making him jump out from it, each day digging the pit a little deeper, until at last he could jump out from a hole which reached almost to his shoulders and up over a wall. And she taught him how to run by chasing him around the tree where they lived, striking at him with a hawthorn switch as they went; until the day came when he could strike at her as they ran, but she could no longer catch up with him.

From the Salmon of Knowledge Cool's son gained his wisdom, and this was the manner of it. One day, on the banks of the Boyne, he came upon an old man fishing. As the boy watched him, the old man caught a fine salmon. Now, this was the Salmon of Knowledge and, as the old man was well aware, there was a prophecy which said that whoever ate the Salmon of Knowledge would gain all the wisdom of the world. The old man handed the fish to the boy, bidding him, 'Cook this for me, but eat no part of it yourself.' The boy made a fire, and spitting the salmon on a stick, cooked it over the embers. But as he was turning it on the spit, he burnt his finger. To ease the smart, he put his finger into his mouth, and so he tasted the fish and acquired wisdom.

Needing arms, he hired himself to an Ulster smith for a year and a day and for his labours earned from the smith a sword which never left a blow unfinished. But it was by his enemies that Cool's son was given a name. When he went amongst them, unknown to them, they asked, seeing his yellow hair, 'Who is the fair one?'

'Now you are named,' said Fleet Foot to him. And from that day on he was known as Finn – the Fair One.

Since he was now tall and strong enough, and skilled enough in feats of arms, and since he now had wisdom, a sword and a name, Finn Mac Cool went to seek out his father's men. He found the Clan Baskin living miserably, hiding in caves along the seashore, with little to eat save shellfish, clad in rags, their hair and their beards unkempt, and with no aim in life save to await the fulfilment of a prophecy which said that one day a son of Cool would come to lead them. They were overjoyed to see Finn. They polished their weapons, trimmed their hair and their beards and made ready to follow him wherever he might lead them.

But first Finn was determined to win the leadership of the Fianna. He went alone to Tara, making his way to the High King's house at a time when Conn was feasting with all his lords and warriors. Finn walked into the king's hall where Conn sat at the high table with his family, while below him, at their long table, sat the warriors of the Fianna, with Gaul Mac Morna, their leader. Quietly Finn laid aside his weapons and without a word he sat down amongst the Fianna. Everyone stared at him, not least the High King himself, and after a moment Conn smiled and said to his cupbearer, 'He is a fine-looking youth, the golden-haired stranger. Take him a cup of wine with my greeting and ask him his name.'

When Finn had received the cup, he stood up and said clearly and loudly, 'I am Finn Mac Cool and I have come to Tara to offer you my service, O king.'

'You are welcome, son of my old friend Cool,' said Conn. 'Come you here and sit by me.'

So Finn went and sat at the high table beside the king, while the Fianna marvelled and Gaul Mac Morna, who had slain Cool, frowned down at the boards of the table.

While they ate and drank and talked at the high table,

Finn learnt that every twelve months, at that time of year, a monster would come to Tara and burn down the walls of the king's house with its fiery breath. No man could withstand this monster, for as it came it played sweet music on a harp, and immediately they heard the sound of this music, all men would fall into a deep sleep, and while they slept the monster might do its will unchecked.

Finn considered this, and, when the feasting was over, he rose and said to Conn, 'If I rid Tara of this monster, will you give me the leadership of the Fianna, which my father had?'

'I will indeed,' said the High King, 'and I call on all those here to bear witness to my words.' And so Finn went out alone on to the walls of the stronghold to await the coming of the monster.

Now, there was in the king's household a man named Fiacha, who had, in the old days, been a follower of Cool. This man now came to Finn carrying a spear of dark bronze, with thirty rivets of gold. 'It is an enchanted spear,' he said to Finn. 'Take it, and when you hear the fairy music of the monster, lay the blade against your brow, and you will not fall asleep.'

Finn thanked him and took the spear and waited in the darkness of the night, walking slowly around the ramparts that encircled the stronghold of Tara. As he went he suddenly caught the first faint sounds of the music of the harp and stopped to listen, entranced by its beauty. Nearer and nearer it came, until all his strength had almost left him and he was half asleep already. Then with an effort he roused himself and lifted the spear, touching his brow with the cool, dark blade. Immediately he was wide awake and no longer under the spell of the music. At the same moment he saw the monster approaching, breathing out flames. With a great cry he rushed at it, flourishing the enchanted spear, and it turned and fled from him. Finn pursued it, flung the spear, and the

monster fell to the ground. Finn cut off its head with his sword, and setting the head on the point of the spear, returned to the king's house.

In the morning Conn of the Hundred Battles called the Fianna together and said, 'Finn Mac Cool has rid us of the menace of the Monster of the Flaming Breath. He is now your leader by right of deed and by right of birth. Those of you who do not wish to obey him, let them go elsewhere.' He turned to Gaul Mac Morna. 'What of you, Gaul? Will you stay and accept Finn's leadership, or will you leave Ireland?'

And tall, squint-eyed Gaul Mac Morna, who, from his mighty sword strokes in battle was known as Gaul of the Blows, hesitated. Then, though it cost him much to speak the words, he said, 'I will accept Finn Mac Cool as leader and stay in Ireland.'

And once Gaul Mac Morna, who had slain his father, had accepted Finn, no one else refused him, and so Finn became leader of the Fianna; and their finest leader he was from that moment until his death.

Finn soon gathered about him a small band of the best warriors of the Fianna, who were his comrades in many an adventure. Second only to Finn in battle-skill and courage was Gaul Mac Morna. Yet though Gaul was often Finn's chosen companion, there was only peace between them, but no love; for neither could forget the death of Cool. Among Finn's other followers were Keelta – Thin One – chief of the Clan Ronan, who could run faster than any other man of the Fianna; bald-headed Conan, quick-tempered and a bit of a braggart, of whom it was said that he never saw a man frown but that he thought it his duty to strike him, and he never saw an open door without going through it. And, later, there were auburn-haired Dermot O'Dyna, the son of Finn's sister, a fine warrior and very handsome; and Finn's own son, Oisin, the great bard of the Fianna, who was the father of Finn's brave grandson, Oscar.

Finn dearly loved red-haired Oscar and greatly mourned his early death. After Oscar had been slain in battle, Finn made this lament for him:

> Best loved of all, O best loved of all,
> Son of my son, slender and fair;
> My heart runs wild and I despair,
> Oscar lies slain to rise no more.
>
> My heart is wrung by Oscar's death;
> Great is our loss, the champion of our land.
> A sword held in a braver hand
> When have I seen in all my days?
>
> Not for husband wept the wife,
> No sister wept for brother dear;
> As many of us as waited there
> We had only tears for Oscar.
>
> All we have would we give indeed,
> I and those who stand around the bier,
> That the wounds of the hero to us most dear
> Had not let out his life.

Besides his friends and followers, Finn had two huge deerhounds, Bran and Skolaun, whom he prized greatly. This is how he first found Bran.

One time Finn and seven of his men went over the sea in search of three young boys who had been stolen away by a giant. They found the children in the giant's house, and entering while the giant was asleep, they were able to bring them safely away. Lying beside the giant's hearth-fire was an enormous hound bitch with her two pups. As well as the children he had come to find, Finn took the two pups before making his way with his companions to their boat on the shore. But they had not gone far out to sea when the giant awoke, and finding the children and the pups gone, sent the hound bitch after the boat. Into the sea leapt the huge creature and swam after the little boat so fast that it seemed as though the sea sparked with red fire on either side of her. Finn could see no way of saving the boat from being over-turned by the hound, and then he had a sudden thought and flung one of the pups into the sea, in the hope that this would distract her. His plan succeeded. The bitch took up her pup and swam back to the shore with it, and so Finn and his comrades reached home safely. The children were restored to their father, and Finn kept for himself the hound pup and named it Bran.

The little pup grew to a fine, large deerhound, and where Finn was, Bran was never far away. It is said that Finn wept but twice in all his life; once was when Oscar died in battle, and the other time was for the death of Bran. Finn and Bran shared several adventures. Here is one of them.

Finn was one day walking on the beach, alone save for Bran, when he saw a boat making for the shore. In the boat were three huge men, far taller and broader than Finn – and he was tall and broad enough, as men are judged. As the boat touched land, the three men jumped on to the sand and strode towards Finn.

'Well,' said one of them, 'and what news for us has the little herd-boy with the dog?'

'I have no news,' replied Finn, 'unless I hear it from the big men who have come from the sea.'

'Our news is that we have come from the Kingdom of the Big Men to look for Finn Mac Cool,' they said. 'Go you and fetch him to us, if you can.'

Finn at once had a great desire to see the country from which these huge men came, so he said, 'Maybe I will fetch Finn Mac Cool and bring him to you, but until I come back,

I bind you to remain here on the shore and do no harm to any man.' With that Finn left them, and going to where there was a little boat a short way off, he put out to sea, taking only Bran with him. Over the sea he sailed until he reached the Kingdom of the Big Men and there he leapt ashore eagerly and made his way inland.

He had not gone very far before he came upon a huge man walking round and round a tree. Finn greeted him, and he asked Finn, 'Well, what news has the dwarf with the lap-dog?'

'I have no news,' said Finn, 'unless I hear it from the big man who is walking around the tree.'

'My news,' said the big man, 'is that for years the king has wanted a dwarf and a little dog, and now at last I have them to take to him.'

'Tell me first,' said Finn, 'why you spend your time walking around a tree.'

'For what else than for firewood?' And with that the big man pulled up the tree by its roots and dragged it after him towards the king's house.

When the king saw Finn and Bran, he was pleased beyond measure. 'Long have I wanted a dwarf and a little dog, and now I have them!' he exclaimed, and made much of them, giving them choice foods to eat and letting them sleep near him, in his own bedchamber. But Finn soon noticed that every night the king arose and went out from his house and only returned at dawn, cold and wet and weary; and one morning he asked him why this should be.

'For what reason should I answer your question?' said the king.

'For no reason at all,' replied Finn. 'Yet for all that, you might as well answer it.'

'What good will it do to me to tell a small man like you?'

'Even a small man can give good counsel,' said Finn.

'Then I will tell you.' The king sighed. 'For seventeen years I have been without rest or sleep, and all because of a monster which comes out of the sea every night to try and take my kingdom from me.'

'Lie you down and sleep tonight, while I go out to meet the monster,' said Finn.

'You will be killed,' warned the king.

'Let you not worry yourself about that,' said Finn. 'You be sleeping while you can.'

So that night the king slept and Finn went down to the shore with Bran and before very long they saw the monster coming fast, its one great eye shining and the sea seething and churning around its immense length. It came from the water and stretched itself out along the shore and stared at Finn with its eye. 'Well,' it said, 'what news has the little man with the small dog?'

'The king is dead,' said Finn, 'and his men have sent me to ask you to keep away this one night, until they have chosen another king to fight with you.'

'Why should I believe what you say, little man?' asked the monster.

'Why should I tell you lies?' retorted Finn. And at that the monster went away.

When the king awoke in the morning, he cried out, 'My kingdom is lost, and my dwarf and my lap-dog are dead.'

'We are here,' said Finn from beside the king's huge bed. 'And your kingdom is not lost.'

The king was overjoyed. 'I do not remember when I last had such rest and sleep,' he said.

'You may have rest and sleep again tonight,' said Finn. And that night, also, he went down to the shore with Bran.

When the monster came it asked, 'And what news has the little man with the small dog tonight?'

'Only that the queen is dead from grief at the death of the

king, and his men ask that you will keep away for this night, also.'

'Why should I believe you?' asked the monster.

'Why should I tell you lies?' retorted Finn.

'Why should you not?' said the monster; but it went.

Again the king was overjoyed when he woke to find his kingdom safe and his dwarf and his lap-dog still with him; and once again on the third night, Finn went down to the shore with Bran.

As before, the monster came and stretched itself along the beach. 'What news has the little man with the dog for me tonight?'

'Only this,' said Finn, 'that it is foolish for so huge a monster as you to be listening, night after night, to lies from such a small man as myself.'

'Is that your news?' asked the monster in great wrath, and with that it leapt upon Finn and they struggled together on the shore. Things went ill for Finn, and after a time he called out, 'Have you forgotten me, Bran?'

Bran rose and padded slowly around the two of them, and then he lay down on the sand again, his head between his paws, watching.

Finn and the monster fought on, and Finn was almost overcome and he cried, 'You have forgotten me tonight, Bran.'

Bran rose and padded slowly around the two of them once more, then he lay down on the sand again, still watching.

Finn and the monster fought on, struggling and wrestling until Finn knew that his strength was spent and he gasped out, 'I can do no more, Bran. It is the end for me.'

At that Bran jumped up and leapt upon the monster's back, tearing its body open; and between them, Finn and Bran put an end to its life. Then Finn hacked off its head and took it to the king's house – for part of the way carrying it and for part of the way rolling it before him, so heavy it was – and there he set it up on a stake before the doorway, with the big eye looking towards the house.

When the king awoke in the morning, he was in great fear and cried out, 'My kingdom is lost and my dwarf and my lap-dog are dead.'

'That is not so,' said Finn. 'And if you do not believe me, look out through your door and see if I lie.'

The king did so, and when he saw the head of the monster, he was hardly able to contain himself for joy. 'Long ago,' he said, 'it was foretold that one day Finn Mac Cool would give rest both to me and to my kingdom. Tell me, little one, are you Finn Mac Cool?'

'I am,' said Finn.

After that Finn sailed home with Bran; and when he reached home he found the three huge men where he had left them, on the beach, still waiting for him to fetch Finn Mac Cool to them.

On another day, when Finn and his companions had been hunting in the hills and they were just making ready to return home, a tall young man who was a stranger to them all, came up to Finn and greeted him.

'Who are you, stranger?' asked Finn.

'I have come from the east and from the west, and I am seeking a master,' replied the young man.

Finn liked the look of the stranger, so he said, 'If you were to take service with me, what reward would you be asking at the end of a year and a day?'

'Only this: that when the year and the day are passed, you will come with me to a feast in the house of the king of Lochlann, bringing with you neither a dog nor a man, neither a beast nor a child, neither a weapon nor any follower but you yourself.'

Finn, who was always ready for an adventure – even a dangerous one in Lochlann where the Norsemen lived – laughed and agreed to the bargain. The young man served Finn well and faithfully for a year and a day, and when the time was up he came to Finn and said, 'Do I now get my payment? Will you come with me to Lochlann as you promised?'

'I will go with you,' replied Finn. To his men he said, 'If I have not returned from Lochlann by the time that a year and a day are passed, let you all come after me to Lochlann and avenge my death.'

Finn's fool was sitting silent and sad by the fire, with no jests left to make, and Finn, seeing him so sorrowful, went to him and asked, 'Do you weep because I am going away alone into Lochlann, poor lad?'

'If you will take advice from me, I have some advice for you,' said the fool.

'It would not be the first time a fool has advised a king,' laughed Finn. 'What is your advice, poor lad?'

'This: take with you Bran's golden chain, for it is neither dog nor man, child nor beast, neither weapon nor follower.'

'I will take it with me,' said Finn, hanging it at his belt. 'And now farewell to you, good fool.'

Finn and the young man from Lochlann travelled a hard road at a great pace, and at last they reached Lochlann and came to the house of the king, and Finn, weary from his long journey, sat down in the king's hall. Yet there he found no welcome and no fine feast awaiting him, but instead the king and all the lords of Lochlann arguing amongst themselves as to what might be the worst and most shameful death they could give to Finn Mac Cool.

'Let us hang him,' said one of them.

'No. Let us rather burn him,' said another.

'It would be better that he should drown,' said yet another.

And so it went on, until at last one man stood up and said, 'None of these deaths is shameful enough for our greatest enemy. But I have in my mind a death that is more shameful by far than any of these. Let us send him into the Great Glen, so that there the Grey Hound may kill him. For, as we know well, the warriors of the Fianna would consider it the greatest shame of all that their leader should be torn by the teeth and the claws of a dog.'

And to this they agreed.

They took Finn to the Great Glen and went a little way with him along the glen, but as soon as they heard the howling of the Grey Hound in the distance, they turned back and left Finn alone. 'We shall wait beyond the glen,' they said, 'out of reach of the Grey Hound. And if you run from the hound, then you will run on to our spears.'

So Finn remained where they had left him, without weapons or armour, and listened to the howls of the Grey Hound coming closer, until at last the creature came in sight. It was a fearsome beast, this Grey Hound which had prowled in the Great Glen for several years past, tearing and devouring any who dared to pass that way. As huge as Bran it was, with burning eyes and long white fangs; and with every snarl it gave, its hot breath scorched the trees and the grass around. Finn's skin, also, was scorched and burnt, until he thought that every moment must be his last. Yet he stood his ground as the hound came closer, until he could hardly even stand for the pain of the burning.

Then suddenly he remembered the advice of his fool, and though it was not a weapon, he took from his belt Bran's golden chain, and holding it high, he shook it at the Grey Hound. Instantly a remarkable change came over the animal. Its snarling ceased, its breath was no longer fiery, its ears pricked up, and it ran towards Finn, wagging its tail. It leaped up and fawned upon him, and licked with its tongue all the sore and burnt places upon Finn's body, healing them immediately.

Then Finn slipped the chain of gold around the neck of the Grey Hound, and with the hound trotting beside him, he walked the length of the glen to the other end. Now, at this other end of the Great Glen there lived an old man and his wife in a little house, and when the old woman saw Finn coming with the Grey Hound at his side, she gave a loud scream of terror and fled into the house.

'What ails you, wife?' asked the old man.

'There is the finest, tallest and handsomest man in all the world coming through the glen, and he has the Grey Hound with him on a leash.'

'Out of all the men in Lochlann and in Ireland, there is only one who could do such a thing,' declared the old man, 'and that one man is Finn Mac Cool. And the leash will be Bran's chain of gold.' And he hurried out to greet Finn.

Finn told the old man and his wife of his adventure, and they made him welcome, saying, 'If you will, stay you with us, until a year and a day are up.' And this Finn did gladly.

When the year and the day were passed, the old woman came running back into the house one morning, crying out in terror and wringing her hands.

'What ails you, wife?' asked the old man.

'There is a great company of men ranged up along the beach and their leader is a red-haired youth.'

Finn sprang to his feet. 'It is the men of the Fianna, led by Oscar.' And taking the Grey Hound with him, he ran down to the shore.

And there indeed were his men, led by red-haired Oscar, and Bran with them, all come to avenge his death. When they saw him alive and well, they gave a great shout of rejoicing which was heard from end to end of Lochlann. And when Bran and the Grey Hound saw one another, they leapt and frolicked about in great gladness, for the Grey Hound was Bran's own brother, born of one litter, the pup which Finn had thrown into the sea when he was escaping from the giant.

The Fianna raged throughout Lochlann, slaying all the warriors of that land and burning their houses, because of what they would have done to Finn. Then they returned home to Ireland in triumph and feasted for a year and a day.

And that is how the Fianna harried Lochlann, and how Finn won Skolaun, his other hound.

*

In Irish tradition, Bran and Skolaun are Finn's cousins, the two children of his mother's sister, who had been changed into a hound bitch by enchantments.

Ian Direach

The Scottish Highlands are rich in good tales of folk heroes; tales which have been told and enjoyed for century after century. The story of Ian, the king's son, is perhaps one of the gayest and most entertaining of them all. It is also one of the best of the many fox stories which are found in the folk-lore of almost all countries.

Although, judged by the standards of today, his conduct is not always quite so upright and honest as his name would have us believe, Ian Direach is a likeable hero – unless, of course, one prefers to consider the resourceful Gillie Mairtean as the true hero of this tale.

THERE was once a king's son in the Western Isles, a fine, handsome youth who was known as Ian Direach – Upright John. He was skilled in all manner of hunting craft, he could play pleasingly upon the harp, and he had a tuneful voice when he sang. His own mother was dead and the king his father had married another wife; but she had little love for her stepson, though she hid this well, under a semblance of kindness.

One day when Ian Direach was out hunting alone in the hills he spied a fine blue falcon flying by. He immediately fitted an arrow to his bow and shot at the falcon. But such was its speed that it was past him in a flash, and his arrow only grazed the tip of one blue wing, so that a shining feather fell to the ground. Ian took it up and stuck it in his belt and returned home.

'What luck had you today in the hills?' asked the king.

'I had little luck,' replied Ian. 'I shot at a falcon, but all I gained was one feather from its wing.' He turned to smile at his stepmother. 'Yet it was a pretty thing and I thought that you might care for it, so I brought it home for you.' And he gave her the blue feather.

Now, the queen was learned in enchantments, and as soon as she saw the feather she knew that it could only have come from the wing of the magical Blue Falcon, whose skill in bringing down game was unmatched by that of any other hawk, and she determined that she would have the Blue Falcon for her own. 'I am setting it on you as a charge which cannot be disobeyed, Ian Direach, that you leave your father's house in the morning and you do not set foot in it again until you bring me the Blue Falcon,' said she.

And little though he liked the idea, Ian had to set off in the morning in search of the falcon. But though he climbed the hill where he had been the day before, and though he searched until sundown, he had no sight of the Blue Falcon; and at dusk, weary and hungry, he sat down beneath a rock, wrapped in his plaid, and sighed to himself, thinking, 'Long will it be before I see my home again, if I have no better luck than this each day.'

As he sat there in the growing darkness, Ian was suddenly aware of a movement in the heather beside him and he looked round and saw in the twilight Gillie Mairtean the fox, carrying in his mouth the foot and the cheek of a sheep.

'Greeting to you, king's son,' said Gillie Mairtean. 'What may you be doing here at this time of the night?'

'I am seeking the Blue Falcon for my stepmother. Without it I dare not return home, for fear of her evil spells.'

'Tomorrow,' said Gillie Mairtean, 'we will go together to

find the falcon, which belongs to the Giant with the Five Heads, the Five Necks and the Five Humps. But for now, let us share this mutton. It is little enough, yet better than nothing.'

So Ian made a fire and they shared the sheep's cheek and the sheep's foot, and afterwards they lay down close together under the rock and slept. And in the morning they set off, Gillie Mairtean leading, making for the house of the Giant with the Five Heads, the Five Necks and the Five Humps.

When the house came in sight, Gillie Mairtean said, 'Let you be going on alone now, Ian Direach, and offering yourself to the giant as a serving-man, to care for his hawks and his hounds. That way you will be given the Blue Falcon to care for, and at the first moment that you can, let you be stealing it away from the giant and running off as fast as your legs can carry you. But mind, see that no single feather of the falcon touches the door of the giant's house as you are leaving it, or it will be the worse for you.'

Ian thanked the fox and went on alone to the giant's house and knocked on the door. The giant opened to him and asked, 'What do you want, stranger?'

'I would take service with you,' said Ian.

'What are you able to do?' asked the giant.

'I can tend hounds and hawks and all manner of beasts.'

'Then come in,' said the giant, 'for I have need of someone to care for my hawks.'

So Ian watched over the hawks of the Giant with the Five Heads, the Five Necks and the Five Humps, and amongst them was the Blue Falcon itself. And so well did Ian do his work that the giant was pleased and thought to himself that with such a trusty young fellow to care for his hawks, he might well go to visit his brothers on the other side of the mountain, leaving Ian to see that no harm came to his house. Accordingly, early one morning, he set off for a day with his brothers, and Ian found himself alone with the Blue Falcon at last. He took the falcon from its perch and set it on his wrist, and very cautiously he unlatched the door of the house. But as soon as the door was open and the light came streaming in, the falcon stretched its wings in the sunshine, and the very tip of one wing touched one of the doorposts, which immediately set up such an outcry that the giant heard it halfway across the mountain and turned round and strode back and was at his house again before Ian had time to run.

'You thief!' roared the giant. 'You were trying to steal my falcon.'

'I was indeed,' admitted Ian, 'and very sorry for it I am, too, but my stepmother has put it upon me not to go home again unless I take her the Blue Falcon for herself.'

Ian expected the giant to strike him dead on the instant, but the giant only stood there, thinking hard. Then he said, 'I have a great fancy for the White Sword of Light that belongs to the Big Women of Jura. Bring it to me, and I will give you my falcon.'

Ian Direach set out, very thankful to be still alive, but none too hopeful about finding the White Sword of Light, since he did not even know where the Big Women of Jura were to be found. All that day he searched, and in the evening, very dejected, he sat down beneath a rock to rest and then, as before, he felt a movement in the heather and there beside him was Gillie Mairtean. 'So you are without the Blue Falcon, Ian Direach?' he said.

'I am indeed,' sighed Ian. 'And what is more, the giant has sent me to fetch him the White Sword of Light which belongs to the Big Women of Jura. If I do this, he says that he will give me the falcon.'

'Then let us be sleeping now, Ian Direach,' said Gillie Mairtean, 'and tomorrow early we will be going down to the seashore and I will turn myself into a boat and carry you to the island of Jura.'

So they lay down and slept, close together, and in the morning they walked down to the shore and there Gillie Mairtean turned himself with no trouble at all into a little boat and Ian stepped into the boat and it carried him over the sea to Jura. There Ian stepped out of the boat on to the beach and Gillie Mairtean became a fox once more. They walked on together a little way before Gillie Mairtean stopped and said, 'Yonder lies the house of the Big Women. Let you be going on alone now and offering yourself to them as a servant. When they find how well you keep things clean and bright, they will give you the Sword of Light to polish. Then, the moment they leave you alone, take up the sword and run. But mind, do not let the sword touch any part of the house as you leave it, or it will be the worse for you.'

Ian thanked Gillie Mairtean and went to the house and knocked on the door and the Big Women – all seven of them – opened the door to him. 'What do you want?' they asked.

'I am looking for work,' said Ian. 'I am a great one for keeping things polished and bright. Would you be wanting anyone to clean and polish for you?'

'We should indeed,' they said, and they let him in.

Ian worked for them, cleaning and polishing their pots and pans, their knives and their ladles, until he had everything so bright and shining that they said to one another, 'Let us give him the Sword of Light to polish, there can be no harm in it.' So Ian polished the White Sword of Light, which never failed in a blow, and well he polished it, too; until at last there came a day when all the seven Big Women were out of the house at the same time, and Ian was alone. Quickly he took up the Sword of Light and opened the door to step outside. But as he was hurrying over the threshold, the tip of the blade touched the lintel which instantly gave such a shout that in less time than it takes to say it, the Big Women were home again, and all seven angry. 'You are stealing our sword !' they screeched.

'Indeed I am, and I am sorry for it,' said Ian. 'But the Giant with the Five Heads, the Five Necks and the Five Humps has promised me that, if I bring him your sword, he will give me his Blue Falcon. And until I can go home with the Blue Falcon for my stepmother, I may not go home.'

The seven women thought this over for a while, then they said, 'We have for a long time now had a mind to own the Yellow Bay Filly which belongs to the king of Ireland. Bring it to us, and we will give you the Sword of Light.'

Ian, very thankful to have got off so lightly, set out to look for the Yellow Bay Filly. But Ireland was far over the sea, and he had no ship to carry him there, so he went to the shore and sat down under a rock and wondered what he could do about it. And while he was sitting there he heard a sound beside him and looked round, and there was Gillie Mairtean.

'And where is the White Sword of Light, Ian Direach?'

'Back in the hands of the Big Women of Jura,' sighed Ian, 'and there it is likely to stay, for they will only give it to me if I bring them the Yellow Bay Filly which belongs to the king of Ireland.'

'In that case you had better go to Ireland without wasting any more time,' said Gillie Mairtean. 'I will be turning myself into a ship and carrying you there.' He did so immediately, and Ian went aboard the ship and away they sailed for Ireland.

As soon as Ian set foot on the shore of Ireland, Gillie Mairtean became himself once more. 'Now,' he said, 'let you be going to the king's house and offering yourself as a groom. With luck he will give you the Yellow Bay Filly to tend. Then, as soon as you can, when everyone is asleep, saddle and bridle her and ride away as fast as you can. But take care that no part of her save her four hooves touches the stable doorway as you ride out.'

So Ian went up to the king's house and asked to speak with the king, and when he had been brought before the king, he offered himself as a groom.

'A groom is what I am needing,' said the king of Ireland.

So Ian was sent to the stables to care for the horses; and amongst them, as he had hoped, was the Yellow Bay Filly which could outstrip the wind. That very night, as soon as the whole household was asleep, Ian saddled and bridled the filly and led her out through the stable door, very carefully. But when she was almost safely out, she gave a swish of her tail and the tip of one long yellow hair brushed against the doorpost which immediately cried out with such a loud voice that everyone in the king's house awoke on the instant and came running.

'Wretch!' said the king of Ireland. 'Is it stealing my filly you would be?'

'It is indeed,' said Ian, 'and very sorry for it I am. But unless I take your filly to the Big Women of Jura they will not give me their Sword of Light, and unless I take the sword to the Giant with the Five Heads, the Five Necks and the Five Humps, he will not give me his Blue Falcon, and until I bring her the falcon my stepmother will not let me go home.'

Ian expected to be hanged on the instant, but the king looked thoughtfully at him for a while, then he said, 'I have a fancy to marry the daughter of the king of France, for I hear she is the loveliest maid in all the world. Bring her here to me and I will give you the Yellow Bay Filly.'

Sadly Ian went down to the shore, and there, as always, was Gillie Mairtean. 'Do not tell me, Ian Direach, that you have failed again?'

'I have indeed,' sighed Ian. 'But the king has promised to

give me his filly if I will bring him the daughter of the king of France for his bride.'

'Come then,' said Gillie Mairtean, 'let us be going to France.' And once again he turned himself into a ship and Ian went aboard and they sailed for France. Landed on the shore of France, Gillie Mairtean, himself once more, said, 'Now, go you up to the king's house and tell him that you have sailed from Ireland and your ship lies wrecked upon the shore, with the crew all drowned and only yourself saved.'

This Ian did, and the king of France said to him, 'I have a mind to see your ship, stranger. Show me where it is.'

So Ian led him down to the shore where Gillie Mairtean was once again a ship, high and dry in the cleft of a rock; and the king's wife and his daughter came with him to take a look for themselves. As soon as they came near it, they heard the sound of music from the ship. 'What sweet music!' exclaimed the princess. 'Take me on board your ship, stranger, that I may hear it the better.'

So Ian led the king's daughter across the rocks and aboard the ship, and while they walked on the deck, listening to the music, the ship slipped slowly out to sea; and by the time that the king's daughter knew what had happened, they were far out of sight of the land.

Angrily she turned to Ian. 'Take me back to France this very moment,' she demanded.

'Lady, I cannot,' said Ian, 'for I must take you to Ireland, that you may be the king of Ireland's wife. For only then will he give me his Yellow Bay Filly which I need if I am ever to get home again.' He saw the downcast looks of the princess and he could not bear them. 'Do not be unhappy, I beg you,' he said. 'The king of Ireland is a mighty king and he lives in a fine large house. He is young and he has great riches. You will not be unhappy as his wife.'

'Maybe not,' she said slowly. 'But I would rather marry you, Ian Direach.' And after that they said no more, for Ian was of one mind with her.

As soon as Ian and the princess had set foot on the shore of Ireland, Gillie Mairtean took his own shape once again. 'Come,' said Ian to the princess with a sigh, 'I must take you to the king.' But Gillie Mairtean said to her, 'Let you wait here on the shore for us, daughter of the king of France.' And immediately he turned himself into a young woman with reddish hair. 'Come, Ian Direach,' he said. 'Let us be going to the king. A fine wife shall I make him I have no doubt.'

When the king of Ireland heard that Ian Direach and a fair maiden were approaching his house, he exclaimed, 'That will be the daughter of the king of France,' and he sprang up and hastened to meet Ian and the princess, calling out that the Yellow Bay Filly should be fetched from the stables, saddled with a golden saddle and bridled with a silver bridle.

'I have brought for you the daughter of the king of France,' said Ian to the king of Ireland.

'She is welcome indeed,' said the king, taking the red-haired maid by the hand. Well pleased, he gave the filly to Ian, who mounted on her back and rode for the shore where the princess was waiting.

But as soon as Ian was well away from the king's house, Gillie Mairtean became himself once more, leapt upon the king of Ireland and bit him, then fled swiftly away to the shore, where he turned himself again into a ship, and carried Ian and the daughter of the king of France and the Yellow Bay Filly across the sea to the island of Jura. Once safely landed, he said to the princess, 'Let you wait here for us with the filly, king's daughter.' Then he turned himself into the likeness of a young bay mare and went with Ian Direach to the house of the seven Big Women.

When the Big Women saw the fine horse Ian had brought them, they made haste to give him the Sword of Light. Ian took the sword and went quickly back to where the princess waited with the filly.

The Big Women were so pleased to have at last the Yellow Bay Filly which they had so long coveted, that they all wished to ride at once; and since none of them would give way to her sisters, they all of them mounted at one and the same time, the eldest on the mare, and the others each upon the shoulders of another. As soon as they were all mounted, Gillie Mairtean galloped off to the top of a high cliff and there he kicked up his heels, put his head between his forelegs, and over the cliff went the Big Women of Jura, and that was the end of them, all seven. Then Gillie Mairtean became a fox and ran for the shore where Ian waited with the princess and the Yellow Bay Filly.

Yet again Gillie Mairtean became a ship and carried Ian and the others over the sea. Once more on shore, he said, 'Let you wait here with the filly and take care of the Sword of Light, king's daughter.' And, turning himself into the likeness of a sharp sword, he bade Ian carry him to the Giant of the Five Heads, the Five Necks and the Five Humps.

As soon as the giant spied Ian approaching with a fine sword in his hands, he took the Blue Falcon and went to meet him. 'You are welcome, Ian Direach, since you come with the White Sword of Light.' He gave Ian the falcon and snatched away the sword. Ian turned and made his way back to the shore with the falcon on his wrist; but the giant stood there before his house, fingering the sword. Then he raised it in the air and swung it round and round above his head, making it whistle through the air, and chuckling with glee, that he had the Sword of Light at last. But Gillie Mairtean, in the shape of the sword, twisted and turned himself, so that with one huge sweep, the giant cut off all five of his own heads at once, and fell down stone dead. Then Gillie Mairtean, himself again, with a bark of triumph, ran back to the others.

'Now let you be riding home, taking your prizes with you, Ian Direach,' he said. 'But remember, when you come in sight of your father's house, see that you hold the Sword of Light with the sharp of the blade to your nose, so that you may shatter the spell which your stepmother will be putting on you.'

Ian Direach thanked Gillie Mairtean and bade him farewell and mounted on the Yellow Bay Filly, setting the daughter of the king of France behind him; and with the Blue Falcon on one hand and the Sword of Light in the other, he made for his father's house. When he came within sight of it, he remembered what Gillie Mairtean had said, and he held the Sword of Light before his eyes, with the edge of the blade towards him, and so he rode through the gates.

From the door of the house his stepmother saw him come, and she ran out to meet him before anyone else, and as she ran she cast a spell on him. 'Become a bundle of dry sticks, my stepson,' she cried. But because the blade of the Sword of Light was towards her, her spell was shattered and turned back upon herself, and she changed instantly into a bundle of dry sticks, while Ian was unharmed.

The marriage of Ian Direach to the daughter of the king of France was celebrated with great rejoicing, and no one missed the queen's company. After his father's death Ian Direach ruled well and wisely for many a year, and he was always happy and fortunate, for he had the Yellow Bay Filly which could outstrip the wind, the Blue Falcon which never missed its prey, the White Sword of Light which never failed in a blow, and the fairest wife in the world; and all this he owed to Gillie Mairtean. And throughout his days there was friendship between him and Gillie Mairtean, and the red fox and his kind might hunt where they would in the Western Isles and take what they pleased, on the orders of Ian Direach the king.

Tam Lin

After a Highland hero, it is only fair to have a hero from the Lowlands. Among the scores of lovely Scottish ballads the story of Tam Lin is one of the loveliest. The theme of the mortal – man or maid – stolen away by supernatural beings is a popular one all over the British Isles, but especially in Scotland and Ireland, where the Celtic traditions of the sidhe, the fairy folk, are strong and lingering. These fairy folk or little people are, of course, all that now remains of the ancient Celtic deities. Carterhaugh is in Selkirkshire.

THERE was an earl in the south of Scotland, and on his lands, at Carterhaugh, there stood a fairy well. The folk that lived near by would never venture there after dark; and if they had to pass the well by day, with eyes that glanced watchfully from side to side they would leave a gift beside the water, a ring, a silver pin or a garment; and all the young maids were warned to keep far from the well, lest there they should meet with the fairy knight, Tam Lin.

Now, this earl had a daughter, a bonny maid named Janet. All her life she had been told that never must she go near the well at Carterhaugh for fear of the fairy knight. And she shuddered to think of Carterhaugh, yet she thought of Carterhaugh often; and though she said nothing of her resolve to anyone, she had long determined that one day she would see the well for herself, come what might.

One June morning early, when the birds were singing and the sun was bright, Janet braided up her hair about her head and kilted her gown above her knees, slipped out from her father's castle alone and ran all the way to Carterhaugh. There she knelt down beside the well and looked in, but nothing could she see save the water, dark and cold. Yet when she looked up again, a moment later, she saw a white horse with golden trappings standing beside the well, where there had been no horse before. She started to her feet, afraid, and half turned to go; but she was a brave maid and before she went she stopped and plucked as a keepsake a bright rose for her gown from the briar bush that grew beside the well.

No sooner had she picked the rose than there before her stood a tall young man, clad all in green and gold, where there had been no man before. 'Why do you pick my roses, lady? And why do you come to Carterhaugh unbidden?'

Janet looked at him, glance for glance, and held her head high. 'Carterhaugh belongs to my father. I shall come and go by Carterhaugh without your leave, if I wish.'

'The roses,' he said, 'are mine, Janet.'

'You know my name,' she said. 'What is yours?'

'I am Tam Lin,' he answered, and he smiled.

And at his smile she forgot to be afraid and she no longer hid her fear behind a mask of disdain. Instead she looked into his grey eyes and smiled at him in return. They sat together on the grass beside the briar bush with its bright roses and talked, and he took her hand in his. All that long summer's day they spent together, and in the evening they parted and Janet went home to her father's castle.

Janet left Carterhaugh that day with her eyes like stars and her feet treading lightly over the heather; but as the weeks and the months went by she grew pale and sad, for she thought she loved a fairy knight.

The women of the castle looked at her and whispered

amongst themselves, 'Bonny Janet has a lover.' And her father's knights looked at her and laughed to each other, asking, 'Is it one of us?' And her father sent for her and looked long at her and said – not unkindly, for he was fond of her – 'It is time you were wed, my child.'

She lifted her head proudly. 'There is not one of your knights whom I would marry, nor any lord that you could name, for my own true love is no earthly man, and him, or none, shall I wed.'

The earl cried out in horror and exclaimed, 'You do not know what you are saying, my child.'

'I know well what I am saying, father, and I will say it again. My true love is a fairy knight. His milk-white horse is shod with silver and with gold, and goes swifter than the wind.' And she stayed to hear no more of his protests, but braided up her yellow hair about her head and kilted her skirts above her knees, and away she went to Carterhaugh, as quickly as she might for her grief.

It was late in the season for roses, but there was yet one left on the briar bush beside the well. Janet plucked it, and there before her stood Tam Lin.

'Why have you picked my last rose, Janet?'

She looked at him long and searchingly. 'Sometimes,' she said, 'sometimes, I have heard, the fairy people will steal away mortals to dwell amongst them. Tell me truly, Tam Lin, are you of the fairy folk or are you a mortal man?'

'I was born grandson to the earl of Roxburgh, but one day as I rode home from the hunting with him, I was thrown from my horse and I fell on fairy ground. The queen of the fairies herself took me to dwell in her land and be her knight.'

At his words, Janet was glad with all her heart; and then she remembered, and said, 'But can you ever be free of the fairy people? Can you ever leave their land?'

'It is you yourself, Janet, who can free me, if you dare. Tonight it is Hallowe'en and at midnight the fairy people will ride abroad. If you will stand here beside the well, you will see them all ride by, and I shall be amongst them. You must run to my horse and pull me from it and hold me close in your arms, no matter what befalls.'

'But in the darkness of the night, how shall I know you from all the others there?' asked Janet.

'First will come the queen of the fairies, riding alone, and after her, her knights. Let the rider on the black horse pass you by, and he who is mounted on the bay. But run to the man on the milk-white steed, for he will be I. You will know me, Janet, for my right hand will be gloved and my left hand will be bare as a sign to you.'

'I shall not fail you,' she promised him.

'But, Janet, have a care, for the fairy people will not lose me lightly. They will turn me in your arms into all manner of strange shapes. Yet do not let me go, or I shall be lost to you for ever. At the last they will turn me into a burning cinder. Then throw me with speed into the water, and I will become a man again. Cover me with your cloak and I shall be out of their sight.'

'I shall not fail you, Tam Lin,' she repeated.

They parted and she went back to her father's castle. And that morning when she left Carterhaugh, walking through the yellowing bracken, her eyes were dark with anxiety and her steps were heavy and slow; but there was a great determination in her heart.

An hour or so before midnight she crept from the sleeping castle and went once more to Carterhaugh. Her heart beat fast, her limbs were deathly cold, and she was sorely afraid. But she pulled her cloak closely around her and thought of Tam Lin. Beside the well she waited for so long that it began at last to seem as though the fairy people would not come that night. Then, a little after midnight, she heard the faint

sound of bridles ringing, coming closer through the silence, and in the darkness she drew back into the darker shadow of the briar bush. And then she saw the fairy people come by, a strange, elfin glow about them. First came the queen of the fairies with her bright beauty shining through the darkness, her golden hair hanging loose over her grass-green mantle, her horse's mane hung with silver bells; and after her came her knights. The first of them on a raven-black horse, and him Janet let pass; the second on a dusky bay, and him, too, Janet let pass. But the third knight rode on a milk-white horse, his right hand was gloved and his left hand was bare. Janet ran to him and clutched hold of him and dragged him from his horse.

A cry of anger went up from the fairy people, but Janet held Tam Lin close in her arms until she felt him shrink in her grasp and saw that she held in her hands a little smooth-skinned lizard which tried to slip through her fingers. But she held it close and would not let it go. The lizard turned to a long and twisting snake that writhed in her grip. Yet still she held it close and would not let it go. The snake became a huge, grim bear, with long, sharp claws which ripped at her. But she twined her hands among its straggling fur and clung to it when it would have wrenched itself from her grasp, and she would not let it go. Then the bear became a roaring lion with sharp fangs and cruel claws, which flung her to the ground. Yet still she held to it and would not let it go. Then the Lion became a red-hot bar of iron, burning the flesh from her hands. But she clasped it close to her and set her teeth against the pain until it became a glowing cinder that she was holding in her hands.

She rose to her feet and staggered to the side of the well and dropped the cinder into the cold, dark water. A cry as of loss went up from the fairy people, and they swirled about her, wailing and clutching at her with ice-cold hands. Then, by the unearthly, elfin light, she saw Tam Lin climb from the well, a naked man. She tore off her cloak and flung it over him, covering him from their sight, and she pulled him down beside the well and held him close in her arms.

All about her the fairy people fell silent, and in the silence the queen of the fairies spoke. 'She who has won Tam Lin for her own has won a goodly husband. She has taken from me the best knight in all my company.' She laughed shrilly and angrily, a fearful sound in the darkness. 'Oh, Tam Lin, had I known how it would be this night, I would have taken out your two grey eyes and given you two eyes of wood.'

And then they were gone, the queen of the fairies and her people, riding away into the night, their bridles jingling, and Janet crouched beneath the briar bush, her lover safe in her arms, a smile on her lips and a great joy in her heart.

IRELAND

Deirdre and the Sons of Usna

Some of the finest stories in the whole world are to be found amongst the ancient legends of Ireland. This first tale, one of 'The Three Sorrows of Storytelling', is probably the most famous of all Irish legends, and unhappy Deirdre has inspired Irish poets and writers for centuries. Within the last sixty years three of the greatest modern Irish writers, Yeats, Synge and James Stephens, all wrote their own versions of her story.

It is interesting to compare this tale with the last one in the book. Although each has as its theme the elopement of young lovers and the vengeance of a deserted bridegroom, the temperaments of the two heroines are strongly contrasted. Deirdre is selfless and devoted, where Grania is imperious and demanding.

Fergus Mac Roy's inability to refuse a feast, turned by King Conor to his own advantage, perhaps needs a word of explanation. In the legends of the Gaelic-speaking peoples, we meet, over and over again, the geis (plural geasa), a compulsion that was laid upon a man from his early years, always to pursue – whatever the circumstances, or even if to his own disadvantage – a certain line of conduct. Sometimes the geis took the form of a prohibition, like the tabu of certain primitive tribes today. Or sometimes the geis was a temporary one, a binding command for a particular occasion, laid upon one person by another. We meet an echo of one such geis in the story of Ian Direach, where his stepmother forbids him to return home without the Blue Falcon; and in

the story of Finn and the sea monster, where he binds the
Big Men to wait for him on the beach until he returns. A
very definite example of the personal and temporary geis is
in the last story in this book, where Grania forces the unwilling Dermot to take her from her father's house by laying
a geis on him.

Irish legend abounds in instances of lifelong geasa laid on
the great heroes. For instance, Dermot O'Dyna might never
enter a house by a side door; Finn Mac Cool might never pass
more than nine successive nights in Allen; Cuchulain always
had to rise before the sun; and Cormac, son of Conor Mac
Nessa, was forbidden to be drawn in his chariot by horses
which were yoked with yokes of ash wood, or to cross dry-
footed over the River Shannon: these geasa were laid on him
at his birth by Caffa the druid.

A T that time when Conor Mac Nessa was king of Ulster, his
chief storyteller, Felim, made a feast for him and for his men,
the warriors of the Red Branch. While they sat at the feast
in Felim's house, word was brought to Felim that his wife
had given birth to a daughter. Caffa the druid, the king's
seer, immediately arose and went out to search for signs from
the clouds and the stars, that he might foretell the future of
the child. When he returned to the hall, he looked grave, and
to those who questioned him, he said, 'Through this child
shall much sorrow come to Ireland, and through her shall
many heroes die.'

At once a number of the warriors of the Red Branch cried
out that the child should be put to death, but Conor would
not have it so. He said, 'No, let her live. Yet let her be reared
far from the homes of men, where she can cause no harm to
any. And then, when she is of an age for marriage, I myself
will take her for my wife, and thus I shall perhaps be able to
prevent this sorrow which Caffa has foretold.'

It was done as Conor said. The child was named Deirdre – Troubler – and in a house high in the hills, she was left in charge of three people only, two old servants, a man and a woman, and Lavarcham, Conor's poetess. And there, in that lonely place, Deirdre grew up into a lovely maiden.

When she was of an age for marriage, one winter morning, looking out through the window of the house with Lavarcham, Deirdre saw a pool of blood upon the snow, where the old man had killed a calf for their meal that day, and a raven alighting by it, to drink the blood.

'The man whom I wed,' said Deirdre, 'must have those three colours about him: the colour of the raven for his hair, his skin the colour of the snow, and the colour of the blood upon his cheeks.'

Lavarcham smiled and answered thoughtlessly, 'There is but one man I know who is of those three colours. He is Naoise, the son of Usna, one of Conor's young warriors.'

'Bring him here to speak with me,' said Deirdre, 'for I shall not be happy until I have set eyes on him, if he is truly as you say.'

'Have you forgotten,' asked Lavarcham, regretting her words, 'that you are promised to the king?'

But Deirdre pleaded with her, and in the end she relented, thinking that there could be little harm in one brief meeting, and she sent for Naoise. The eldest son of Usna was indeed as Lavarcham had said, with hair like the raven's wing, skin like snow, and cheeks as red as blood. And so far from there being no harm in a single meeting, the moment that they saw one another, Naoise and Deirdre fell in love.

'Never, never will I marry King Conor, now that I have seen you,' said Deirdre. 'Let us fly from here together.'

So Deirdre and Naoise and his two brothers, Ainnli and Ardan, with their men, fled from Ulster. But there was no one in all Ireland who would give them shelter, for fear of

Conor's wrath; and after wandering from place to place, they crossed the sea to Scotland, and there the three brothers took service with the king. But even then there was no peace for them, for the king of Scotland saw Deirdre and wished to have her for his wife, and would have slain Naoise to win her. So once again the sons of Usna were forced to flee. They went to one of the lonely islands off the western coast of Scotland, and there they lived in a little house which they had built themselves.

In Ireland, King Conor sat in his house at Emain Macha and thought of Deirdre, whom Naoise had stolen from him, and his anger and his jealousy grew with every day that passed; yet he hid his thoughts from other men and said instead, 'I have a fine house and great riches, and the best of warriors to serve me, yet those three who are perhaps the best of all, are no longer with us. Let word be sent to the sons of Usna that I forgive them for what they have done, and would willingly welcome them back amongst the warriors of the Red Branch.' He called to him Fergus Mac Roy, the truest and most honourable of all men, and bade him go to Scotland and bring home Deirdre and the sons of Usna. 'Tell them that I have forgiven them and that they may come in safety, fearing no harm, for you will be their surety, good Fergus. Yet I am eager to see them again, so give me your word, Fergus, that once they have set foot in Ireland, whether it is night or day, the sons of Usna will tarry for nothing, neither for eating nor for sleeping, but will come with all speed to Emain Macha.'

'I pledge you my word that it shall be thus,' said Fergus, and with his two sons, Illan the Fair and Buinni the Red, he went gladly to fetch back Naoise and Ainnli and Ardan, whom he had ever greatly loved.

But as soon as Fergus was gone from Ireland, Conor sent for Borrach, whose house stood high on the cliff above the harbour, and he ordered him to prepare a feast for Fergus against his return from Scotland. 'When you see him set foot upon the shore, Borrach, go down to him at once and invite him to the feast,' said Conor; and this Borrach promised to do. Conor smiled to himself, for he knew that Fergus Mac Roy was under bonds never to refuse a feast; and in this way, Deirdre and the sons of Usna would be forced to come alone to Emain Macha, without his protection.

When Fergus landed on the island where the sons of Usna dwelt, he gave a great shout to warn them of his coming. Deirdre and Naoise were sitting at chess in their house, and hearing the shout, Naoise looked up and said, 'That is the shout of a man of Ireland.'

But Deirdre, who had known it as the shout of Fergus Mac Roy, said quickly, 'No, it is the shout of a man of Scotland.'

After a while Fergus gave a second shout, and Naoise said, 'It is indeed the shout of a man of Ireland.'

'It is not,' said Deirdre. 'Let us play our game, Naoise.'

But when Fergus gave a third shout, Naoise jumped to his feet and said, 'That is the shout of Fergus Mac Roy.' And he sent Ardan down to the shore to meet him.

Joyfully Ardan greeted Fergus and his sons, and joyfully he brought them to his brothers and to Deirdre. Naoise and Ainnli embraced their old comrades, and Fergus gave them Conor's message. 'Now let the four of you come back with me to Ireland as soon as may be, for I am your surety,' urged Fergus.

The sons of Usna were glad, but Deirdre said, 'No, let us not go, for I have had a dream. In my dream I saw three birds flying to us from Emain Macha, and in their beaks were three drops of honey which they gave to us: but they took away with them three drops of our blood. Do not trust Conor's message, for sweet as honey are the words of a man who smiles while he meditates on blood and vengeance.'

'I have pledged myself to keep you safely, you have naught
to fear,' said Fergus. 'Though all the men of Ireland should
go against you, yet still I should be your shield.'

'In spite of that,' said Deirdre, 'let us remain in Scotland.'
And she put forward every reason she could, why they
should not go.

Yet Naoise said, 'How can we fear if Fergus is our surety?
Fergus is the best and truest of men and would never betray
us into a trap. We shall go back to Ireland with him.' And
to this his brothers agreed.

And so, for all Deirdre's pleading, the sons of Usna went
from their island with Fergus. And as they went, Deirdre
made her farewell to Scotland.

> Very dear to me is that eastern land,
> Scotland with its wonders.
> I would not have left it
> Had I not followed Naoise.
>
> Kil-Cuan, Kil-Cuan,
> Where Ainnli would wander;
> How short seemed the time to me
> That I spent with Naoise in Scotland.
>
> Glenlee, Glenlee,
> Where I slept beneath the cliffs;
> Fish and venison and badger-flesh
> Have I eaten in Glenlee.
>
> Glen Massan, Glen Massan,
> Where tall grow the white-stalked flowers;
> There were we rocked to sleep,
> In the grassy harbour of Glen Massan.
>
> Glen Etive, Glen Etive,
> Where my first home was built,
> Lovely its woods in the early morning;
> A cage for the sun was Glen Etive.

Glendaruel, Glendaruel,
I remember your people with friendship.
Sweet was the call of the cuckoo
From the bending bough on your peak.

Very dear to me is Draigen,
Its clear waters and its pale sand.
Oh, I would not have left Scotland
Had I not come with my lover.

In Ulster, from his house on the top of the cliff, Borrach was watching for them, and as soon as they had set foot on the shore, he hastened down to meet them, bidding them come to his house to a feast that was prepared for them. Fergus was distressed. He said to Naoise, 'I gave my word to Conor that you would go straight to Emain Macha and tarry nowhere on the way, either to eat or to sleep.'

'Then as you have promised we shall do,' said Naoise. 'What of it? Is missing a feast so hard? Come, Fergus, let us hurry to Emain Macha.' And he made to go on.

But Fergus said, 'If you go to Emain Macha, you must go alone, for I am under bonds never to refuse a feast, and now Borrach has offered me a feast at a most evil moment.'

Neither Naoise nor his brothers answered him, but Deirdre said, 'It were better by far, Fergus, that you should forsake a feast than that you should abandon the sons of Usna whose safety lies in your pledge.'

'A warrior may not forsake his bonds,' said Fergus unhappily. 'I must remain in Borrach's house until the feasting is done. Yet I will send my two sons with you to Emain Macha.'

At this Naoise turned away from him in anger. 'We can defend ourselves. We do not need your sons. Come, my brothers.' And he went from Borrach's house with Ainnli and Ardan and Deirdre and their men. But Illan and Buinni, the two sons of Fergus, followed them, as their father bade them.

The sons of Usna took the shortest road to Emain Macha, but when they were about an hour's journey away, Deirdre stopped and pointed up into the sky. 'See, Naoise, how that cloud yonder glows red as blood. It foretells disaster to us. Come, let us turn aside and ask shelter of young Cuchulain at Dun Dalgan until Fergus has finished his feast and can come with us to Conor's house.'

'We cannot do so,' said Naoise. 'It would be to show fear, and we are not afraid.'

So they went on; and when Conor's house came in sight, Deirdre said, 'I will know for sure what Conor means towards us by his manner of receiving us. If he welcomes us himself and bids us sit at his table and eat with him, we are safe, for no man would kill the guest who shares his meat. But if he sends us to feast in the house of the warriors, then he means us no good.'

The sons of Usna called loudly outside Conor's gate and Conor's porter came out to them. 'Go, tell the king,' said Naoise, 'that here are the sons of Usna and the sons of Fergus, waiting at his door.'

The porter went to Conor and told him, and Conor asked his servants, 'Is there food and drink enough in the House of the Red Branch for the sons of Usna and the sons of Fergus and their men?'

'There is food and drink enough for seven battalions of Ulstermen,' he was told.

'Then take the sons of Usna and the others to the House of the Red Branch,' said Conor.

When Deirdre heard that they were to go to the warriors' house, she said, 'There is still time to fly. Let us go while we are yet alive.'

But Illan the Fair answered her, 'We have shown no fear until now. Would you make cowards of us all?'

And Deirdre was silent, and went with them into the House of the Red Branch, where food and drink were brought to them. They laid aside their weapons and feasted, all save Deirdre and the sons of Usna, for the four of them knew well their end was near and they had no heart for feasting. Then Naoise asked for a chessboard, and when it had been brought, he and Deirdre sat down to play.

In the king's house Conor sat at the high table, and as he ate and drank he thought of Deirdre and the sons of Usna; and at last he called Lavarcham to him and said, 'Go now to the House of the Red Branch and bring me back news of Deirdre, whether she is still lovely to look upon.'

Lavarcham went to the House of the Red Branch and greeted Deirdre and kissed her. Then she wept and said, 'Evil are the deeds that Conor plans. Bar the door and shutter the windows when I am gone, and, if you can, keep all Conor's men at bay until Fergus comes.' With that she returned to Conor, and the sons of Usna barred the door after her and fastened the shutters over the windows.

To Conor Lavarcham said, 'I have seen Deirdre, my king, and she is not as she was in the days that are past. Her hard years of wandering in Scotland have brought lines to her once lovely face, and her eyes are no longer bright.'

And Conor thought, 'If that is so, I do not want her. Let Naoise keep her.' And he turned again to his eating and drinking.

But after a time it came into his mind that Lavarcham might have lied to him, so he called to Trendorn, who had always hated the sons of Usna, and bade him go to the House of the Red Branch and bring him word of Deirdre.

When Trendorn came to the warriors' house, he found the door barred and the windows shuttered; but he spied a small window high in the wall, and he climbed up and looked down into the hall and saw Deirdre and Naoise playing at chess.

While she was waiting for Naoise to make a move, Deirdre glanced upward and saw Trendorn at the little window. She grasped Naoise's arm and said to him, 'Look, above us, there is someone watching.' Naoise looked up and saw Trendorn, and taking one of the chessmen, he flung it at him with such true aim that he put out Trendorn's eye.

In pain and anger Trendorn returned to Conor. 'The three sons of Usna sit in the warriors' hall like three kings, and Deirdre sits beside them. And she is the loveliest woman in all Ireland,' he said.

Immediately Conor arose, in a great rage of jealousy, and he called for his hireling warriors – since he knew well that none of the warriors of the Red Branch would take arms against the sons of Usna – and he bade them bring forth Naoise and his brothers from the warriors' hall. With shouts the hirelings attacked the house, but the doors stood firm; so they laid faggots and kindling around the walls and set fire to them.

Inside the house, Buinni the Red rose up. 'I stand in my father's place as your pledge of safety. Mine is the right to drive off these attackers.' He opened the door and went out with his followers, scattering or killing many of Conor's men, and stamping out the flames. But when it was done, he did not return to Naoise, for Conor sent to him, offering him great gifts if he would break his word to the sons of Usna, and this Buinni did.

Then Conor's men attacked again, and Illan the Fair said, 'My brother has betrayed you, yet I also stand in my father's place as your pledge of safety. I will go out to meet your enemies, and be assured that I shall not sell you to King Conor.' Followed by his men, Illan went out and drove off the attackers. But Illan, too, like his brother, did not return, for he was slain in the fighting.

It was now evening, and darkness was falling, but the

hireling warriors came again and again to the fight. The sons of Usna divided the night into three parts and each kept guard over one third of the night, first Ardan, then Ainnli, and lastly, towards dawn, Naoise. And when the sun rose, Naoise, weary and spent with fighting, looked out across the slain, both friends and foes, who lay before the House of the Red Branch, and he saw, a little way off, Lavarcham watching the battle anxiously, and he called to her, 'Go upon the walls, Lavarcham, and see if Fergus and his men are in sight, for we have great need of them.'

Lavarcham went; but heavy at heart she came back and called to him, 'I can see naught but the cattle grazing on the plain, Naoise. Fergus is not coming yet.'

'There are too few of us to hope to hold the house any longer,' said Naoise to his brothers. 'Let us try to fight our way out of Emain Macha.'

So, setting Deirdre in the midst of them, with their shields and spears as a wall about her, the sons of Usna and their few remaining men fought a way out through their enemies. And so bravely they fought that they might well have broken away and escaped with their lives, had not Conor, seeing that he was likely to lose them, tricked them yet again. He sent for Caffa the druid, saying, 'Go, tell the sons of Usna that if they will lay down their arms and submit to me, I will not hold it against them that they have slain so many of my men. Instead I will restore them to their honoured place among the warriors of the Red Branch.'

When they heard Conor's offer from Caffa, the sons of Usna threw down their weapons and went gladly to him to make their submission, but Conor ordered them bound; and when it had been done, he called out, 'Who will slay these traitors for me?'

There was not one among the men of Ulster who would do so foul a deed for him; but a man from Norway, Maini of the

Red Hand, stepped forward saying, 'I will do it for you, lord.'

'Let me die first, I am the youngest,' begged Ardan, for he did not wish to see his brothers die.

Ainnli, too, could not bear to watch his brothers slain, and he said, 'I was born before you, Ardan, therefore I should die first.'

But Naoise said, 'My sword was given to me by Manannan Mac Lir, the sea god, and it never leaves a stroke unfinished. Let Maini use it and strike off all our heads at once.'

The three sons of Usna bent their necks close together, and Maini of the Red Hand took up the sword and with one blow he struck off all three heads.

Deirdre flung herself down beside the dead brothers, tearing her golden hair in her grief; and she wept and spoke a lament over them.

'The three lions of the hill are dead,
The three sons of a king who ever made strangers welcome.

The three hawks of Slieve Gullion,
The three sons of a king who were served by many warriors.

It was joy to be with Naoise and Ainnli and Ardan.
My life will not last long now that they are gone.

O you who dig the grave for the sons of Usna,
Let it be wide and deep enough, that I may lie beside them.'

Then her heart broke and she lay down by Naoise and died.

*

Manannan Mac Lir, the sea god, who gave Naoise his sword, is one and the same as the Welsh hero, Manawyddan, son of Llyr, in the story of Bran and Branwen. Manannan gave his name to the Isle of Man, where he is still said to bring down the mists which periodically veil the island.

Cuchulain, the Hound of Ulster

Many nations have their own matchless young hero who dies while still at the height of his youth, yet achieves undying fame. Often he is, in some way or another, offered the alternative of a short life and lasting fame, or a long life and oblivion, and deliberately makes the choice of an early death himself. The Greeks had Achilles, the Germans, Siegfried, and the Irish, Cuchulain.

Cuchulain, like the Arthurian Gawaine, is a solar hero. As the child of the sun god Lugh, he is himself an aspect of the sun. We are told that though in peaceful moments he was small and insignificant in appearance, in battle he grew in stature; and when he was at his full strength, no one might look him in the face. The solar connexion is there quite obvious. In the fourteenth-century story of Sir Gawaine and the Green Knight, Gawaine, alone of all Arthur's knights, is courageous enough to accept the challenge of the terrifying stranger to exchange blows with him – Gawaine to strike off his head there and then and the challenger to strike off Gawaine's head when next they meet. An almost identical tale is told of how Cuchulain, alone of the Red Branch warriors, accepts a similar challenge and passes through the test triumphantly, to find the monstrous stranger was his former host in magic guise. The accretions of medieval chivalry found in the story of the Green Knight are missing in the Cuchulain version, but nevertheless it is the same story, told of the two solar heroes.

The arch-enemy of the Red Branch warriors, proud Maeve of Connaught, who had many husbands in succession – she had once been married to King Conor and had left him through her great pride – must surely have originally been more than mortal: a Mother Goddess perhaps, or, as some scholars have suggested, the personification of sovereignty, which a king may be said to wed symbolically on his accession. The Gaelic spelling of her name is Medb – the pronunciation is the same as in the anglicized form – and it is probably Maeve who survives through the Middle Ages and on into Shakespeare's day as Queen Mab of the fairies.

In the course of the calamitous Cattle Raid of Cooley, Maeve's questions to Fergus at the approach of Conor's army, and his replies, bring to mind the questions of Matholwch's swineherds and the answers of Branwen.

IN the days when King Conor Mac Nessa ruled in Ulster, his half-sister Dectera, daughter of Caffa the druid and seer, a fair maiden who was betrothed to Sualtach, one of Conor's lords, was stolen away by Lugh of the Long Arm, the sun god. For months Conor and his warriors searched for her, and when they at last found her and she returned in their company to Ulster, she brought with her Setanta, her child and Lugh's. Sualtach and Dectera were married, and when he was old enough, Setanta went to the king's house at Emain Macha to be brought up with the sons of the other Ulster chiefs and lords who were being trained as warriors at Conor's court. Though small and slight, Setanta was as strong as any boy of twice his years, and he soon became the leader of Conor's troop of boys.

One day when Setanta was seven years old, Conor and all his lords were invited to a feast in the house of Culann, the smith who forged the finest of weapons for the king and his

Red Branch warriors. As they left the stronghold of Emain Macha on their way to the feast, they passed by some of the boys who were playing hurley, Setanta alone against twelve others. King Conor stopped a while to watch the game, and he was so pleased at the skill shown by Setanta that, before he moved on, he called out to the boy, bidding him follow them to the feasting. But Setanta delayed long enough to finish – and win – the game, so that when he started off along the track to Culann's house, it was to find that the king and his men were out of sight. He ran after them, but by the time he reached the smith's house they were all inside and sitting at the feast, and the gate was barred fast.

Now, Culann kept no porter at his gate, for he had a huge wolfhound to protect his home and needed no other guard. This meant that there was no one to open the gate to Setanta or even to hear him when he called out. So, undaunted, he climbed the big wooden gate and jumped down into the courtyard the other side. Instantly, baying furiously, the hound leapt at him. Setanta flung his hurley stick at the beast and then grabbed it by the throat, and lifting it with all his strength, he dashed its head against the gatepost, killing it.

At the sound of the hound's baying, Culann and all his guests had risen, and now they hurried out into the courtyard. When they saw little Setanta standing there, beside the body of the huge hound, Conor exclaimed, 'That was a brave feat. Truly, one day that boy will be accounted among the greatest of my Red Branch warriors.'

But Culann was sad and angry at the death of his good hound which had died defending its master's house, and seeing this, Setanta went to him and said, 'It was to save my life that I killed your hound, but I give you my promise that I will find you another hound as good, and train it as a watch-dog to guard your house for you. And until then I myself shall be your hound and guard your home.'

And from that day Setanta was known as Cuchulain – the Hound of Culann.

One morning, not long after, Cuchulain overheard Caffa the druid say to some of the older youths in Conor's troop of boys, that the boy who was given arms on that very day would become one of the greatest warriors in all Ireland, but that his life would be short and hard. Cuchulain instantly went to Conor and asked the king to give him arms. Conor smiled at him and granted his request, giving him light weapons fitted to his age and size. Taking the spears in his hands, Cuchulain snapped the shafts in half, one after the other, and likewise he broke the sword. Conor gave him two stronger spears and a heavier sword, but these, also, Cuchulain broke. And so it was with all the weapons that Conor gave to him; until the king sent for two spears and a sword which had been made for his own use, fine weapons, strong and heavy, and these Cuchulain could not break and he was satisfied at last.

After this young Cuchulain had several bold adventures. He captured and mastered two horses which rose from the depths of a lake, the Grey of Battle – for ever after his favourite horse – and the Black of the Glen, and yoked them to his chariot; and he slew three fierce enemies of Ulster.

Besides this, he travelled many miles to the home of Scatha on the Isle of Skye, for Scatha was a famed warrior-woman and from her he learned much skill. In Skye, too, he made his greatest friend, Ferdia, a youth from Connaught, who was one of several other lads who were training in skill of arms with Scatha. Cuchulain, who was the younger, served as Ferdia's attendant, taking care of his weapons for him and carrying his spear when they hunted together. A deep affection soon grew between the two of them and they were never parted from each other for all the years they both remained on Skye.

The fame of Cuchulain's feats travelled fast and far, and by the day that he was no more than seventeen years old, his praises were on all men's lips and his name was known throughout all Ireland.

At that time Queen Maeve with her husband Ailell ruled in Connaught. Maeve, daughter of the High King of Ireland, was both beautiful and proud; so proud that she resented even her husband's riches and authority. One evening the two of them began to boast of their wealth and power. Ailell spoke of his many warriors: Maeve reminded him of her own. Ailell numbered his servants and bondsmen: Maeve had as many. All night they spent in reckoning the sum of their chariots and their horses, their flocks and their herds, their jewels and their weapons, their brazen cauldrons and their silver drinking cups, even the cooking utensils in their kitchens. And in all things their possessions were equal, save in one thing alone: Ailell had amongst his cattle the famed White-horned Bull of Connaught, and Maeve had no bull the equal of this fine beast. Vexed by this, Maeve sent for her herald in the morning and asked him if anywhere in Ireland there might be a bull the equal of the White-horned.

'There is, my queen,' he replied. 'Dara of Cooley, in Ulster, owns such a bull. The Brown Bull of Cooley is the equal in every way of the White-horned.'

'Go to Dara,' commanded Maeve, 'offer him gifts and ask him to lend me his bull for the space of one year.'

In Ulster Dara received Maeve's messengers kindly and at once agreed to lend her his bull. But in the feasting that he made for his guests he overheard one of the Connaught men, who had drunk more than was wise when among strangers, brag that had Dara not lent his bull willingly, Queen Maeve would have come and taken it by force.

This angered Dara and he cried out, 'Let her come and

take my bull then, if she dare!' And he sent the messengers away empty-handed.

When she heard his answer, Maeve at once called together her warriors and sent heralds throughout Ireland to summon her allies to Connaught. When the huge army was gathered, she set herself at its head, and under her – because he knew the tracks and fords of his own land – Fergus Mac Roy, who had left Ulster and the service of King Conor after the killing of the sons of Usna. Moreover, Maeve chose well the time at which to make her attack against Ulster, for, because of the anger of a goddess many years before, there was a spell upon the warriors of Ulster, that for a certain season each year, as winter was beginning, they would lose all their strength, become as helpless as new-born babes, and fall into a deep sleep. At the time when Maeve's great army was ready to march, this strange sickness was once again due, and Maeve believed that there would thus be no one to protect Ulster from her attack.

As she set out, Maeve asked her chief druid, 'How shall I prosper in this raiding?'

'Who comes or comes not back to Connaught, O queen, you will come,' he answered.

'Can you see the men of my army in the battle?' asked Maeve of her prophetess.

'I can see them,' said the woman, 'and they are coloured red.'

'How so?' demanded Maeve, surprised. 'Is not the spell of the goddess on the warriors of Ulster at this very moment?'

'I see them red, your men,' repeated the prophetess. 'Against them I can see but one champion, young and beautiful. Small he is, and slight; a little warrior, but very fierce in battle. And I see your men all red, O queen.'

Maeve was perturbed, but shrugging her shoulders, she mounted into her chariot and led her army towards Ulster.

For all the wrong done to him by King Conor, Fergus Mac Roy was heavy at heart at the thought of the sorrow that would soon fall upon Ulster and upon his one-time comrades of the Red Branch, and he secretly sent a messenger to Emain Macha with a warning of the danger that was coming. But Conor and his warriors had all been stricken by the sickness, and, of them all, Cuchulain, as the son of a god, was alone untouched by the spell. And so it was that it fell to Cuchulain to defend the borders of Ulster unaided against Queen Maeve, and to hold back the men of Connaught and their allies and harry them as best he could, until the spell had lifted once again from King Conor and the Red Branch warriors.

Cuchulain bade red-haired Laegh, his charioteer, yoke the Grey of Battle and the Black of the Glen to his chariot, while he himself gathered up his weapons, sword and spears and the Gae Bolg, his barbed javelin that never failed to slay; and then he drove swiftly southwards. He went to the ford of the river where Maeve's army would have to cross on its way into Ulster, and there he was seen by two scouts who had been sent forward by the queen. Both these men he slew, and their charioteers, also. Then he cut down a forked sapling, stripping it of its twigs, and drove it deep into the bed of the river in the middle of the ford, writing his name in secret letters on a piece of bark which he fastened to the pole, and on each fork of this pole he put a severed head. So that when Maeve, driving before her army, reached the ford, the first thing that she saw was the heads of her two scouts and their charioteers, set up in the midst of the river.

'In spite of the spell, the men of Ulster have raised an army to meet us,' she said. And she sent for Fergus to question him.

But Fergus saw Cuchulain's name in the secret letters, and he said, 'That is the work of young Cuchulain. Many will be the men of Connaught and their allies who will regret coming forth against Cuchulain, before this raiding is over.'

Maeve and her army advanced into Ulster, and Cuchulain, from the cover of the forest, or hidden behind rocks and bushes, harried her continually, both in camp and on the march, giving her no peace while daylight lasted; even killing, with stones from his sling, Maeve's pet bird as it perched on her shoulder and a tame squirrel on her knee, as she sat, safe in the midst of her camp, before her tent. And even after darkness, too, the enemies of Ulster might not sleep in peace, for by night Cuchulain would creep upon the camp and slay as many as a hundred men before slipping swiftly away. And, too, the winter was by now upon them, and sometimes the snow was halfway up their chariot wheels as they went on their way.

More than once Maeve sent to Cuchulain with offers of great gifts and her friendship if he would desert King Conor, but he scorned to consider her bribes. Yet at last Fergus Mac Roy, who had been his good friend in Emain Macha when he had been a child, persuaded him to leave his harrying of Maeve's army and to fight instead with one picked champion each day. It was agreed that so long as the fight between the two of them lasted, the army would march on into Ulster, but the moment the Connaught champion fell, the army would pitch camp until the next day. For, as Maeve thought, it would be better to lose one man every day – even though he might be a fine warrior – than to lose a hundred lesser men every night.

So she offered rewards, great riches and the hand of her young daughter, to the man who would bring her Cuchulain's head; and every morning, while the army marched on into Ulster, a champion would fight with Cuchulain. But he slew every one of them, and so quickly that the army advanced no more than a little distance each day. Then Maeve in despair broke her word and sent one warrior after another to fight with Cuchulain as long as the daylight lasted, so that he had no rest from fighting. But, wounded and weary though he was, no one of all the champions of Connaught or of Maeve's allies who came against him, was a worthy adversary for him, and he slew them all.

And indeed, in all Maeve's army there were but two men who could have held their own for long against Cuchulain, and those two were Fergus Mac Roy and Ferdia, the young Connaught warrior with whom Cuchulain had learnt battle skill from Scatha and who was his much loved friend: and neither of these two, for all Maeve's promises and entreaties, would fight against Cuchulain, whom they loved.

But while Cuchulain fought with champion after champion, unknown to him, Maeve sent a band of men in search of the Brown Bull of Cooley. They found and captured the bull near Slieve Gullion and drove him off towards Maeve's camp. Cuchulain had word of this and pursued them and challenged and slew their leader. But while he fought, the other men in the band hurried southwards with the bull, out of Cuchulain's reach, and disappointed and dispirited he abandoned the pursuit. Maeve had achieved her desire and Cuchulain had been unable to prevent her.

But the war was not yet over. Queen Maeve had gathered together too great an army and had tempted too many allies to her side with promises of booty, for them to be content with seeing their leader win the Brown Bull for herself, while they gained nothing. So the fighting went on.

As Cuchulain, weary, disconsolate and wounded, sat huddled by his lonely camp fire one evening, with Laegh at his side, Lugh of the Long Arm came to him and put a deep sleep upon him. In this sleep, which lasted for three days and nights, the sun god healed his wounds and filled him with new strength.

While Cuchulain slept, Ulster was unguarded; but Conor's

troop of boys – on whom the spell of the goddess had no power, since they were not yet men – came out from Emain Macha, one hundred and fifty of them, and, led by a young son of the king, they attacked Maeve's great army on each of the three days. Three times they attacked, and with every attack they killed their own number of the enemy; but at the last they all lay dead.

When Cuchulain awoke from his sleep, refreshed and whole again, and learnt that Conor's boys had died defending Ulster, he leapt to his feet, moved by pity and great anger and called to Laegh, 'Make ready the chariot, for I will avenge them.'

Round and about Maeve's camp he drove in vengeance, and through the ranks of her men, the scythes on the wheels of his swift chariot mowing down the hapless men like grass and leaving the dead piled high behind him on the plain. And so, in the great Slaughter of Murthemny, Cuchulain avenged the youths of Ulster.

Maeve, appalled by the loss of so many of her men, urged Fergus ever more strongly to challenge Cuchulain. 'I have given you the leadership of my army,' she said, 'and you shame me and yourself by your inaction.'

So at last Fergus went to meet Cuchulain : but he went without his sword.

'Fergus,' said Cuchulain, 'you are not wise to come to me without your sword.'

'If I had it with me, I would not use it against you,' replied Fergus. 'I do not want to fight you, Cuchulain, but I can bear Maeve's reproaches no longer.' He paused and thought a while, then said, 'Let us pretend to fight, Cuchulain, and let you turn and run from me, so that Maeve is satisfied. Then, when we next meet in battle, I will flee from you.'

To this Cuchulain agreed, and they fought for a short while and then Cuchulain gave way before Fergus and turned and fled from him in the sight of Maeve and all her men; and Fergus returned to the queen, having done as she bade him, so that she could no longer reproach him.

But Maeve wanted Cuchulain dead, so she sent for Ferdia and renewed her offers to him. 'I will not fight against my friend,' said Ferdia, 'not for your goodwill, not for all your gifts, not even for your lovely daughter.'

Maeve frowned. 'Then I shall have my bards make songs about you, so that you will be known throughout all Ireland and until the end of time as the warrior who was afraid to face one man alone, and he not over tall.'

'That would be unjust,' said Ferdia, 'and a lie.'

'Nevertheless,' said Maeve, 'that is how it will be, and that is how men yet unborn shall remember Ferdia, son of Daman, unless you do this thing for me.'

Sadly and slowly Ferdia went from her, and in the morning he mounted his chariot and drove to the River Dee, where Cuchulain held the ford. At the ford Cuchulain was waiting. When he saw that it was Ferdia coming towards him, he said, 'I never thought to have to fight against you, Ferdia, my friend.'

'In spite of that, I have come,' said Ferdia, 'so take up your weapons.'

All that day they fought, sending their light spears over the river, time after time. But they were so well matched that neither wounded the other, and it was almost as if they were once again at practice, watched by Scatha on the Isle of Skye. And when dusk fell, with one accord they cast down their weapons and ran towards each other and, meeting half-way across the ford, they flung their arms about each other. When they parted, each to go to his own side of the river, Ferdia sent across to Cuchulain half of the food and drink brought to him from the camp; and all that night Laegh sat at one fire with Ferdia's charioteer, and the Grey of Battle and the Black of the Glen were tethered beside the horses of Ferdia.

In the morning the combat went on. This time they fought from their chariots with their heavy spears, and so good was their aim and so well matched they were, that by sunset each was sorely wounded. Yet when they dropped their weapons, each climbed wearily from his chariot and started across the ford, and in the middle they met and once again they kissed before they went to rest. And once again Ferdia shared his supper with Cuchulain, while Cuchulain sent to Ferdia half of his store of healing ointments and herbs; and once again, too, their charioteers sat together, and their horses were watered and foddered side by side.

But in the morning Cuchulain looked over the river and saw Ferdia's dejected mien as he armed himself, and he crossed the ford to him. 'Let us end this fight, Ferdia, before one of us kills the other.'

Sorrowfully Ferdia shook his head and turned away. 'It is too late. I cannot cease now without losing my honour for ever. I am not afraid to die. It is Maeve, not you, who will have destroyed me.'

When he saw that he could not persuade his friend, Cuchulain left him and returned sadly to the northern bank of the river; and all that day they fought again, their weapons flying back and forth across the stream until evening came, when they let their weapons fall from their hands and turned away without a word. That night their horses were tethered apart, and their charioteers had each his own fire.

In the morning they arose and put on their full armour and laid ready all their weapons, for both knew that this day would see the ending of their fight. With their swords in their hands they strode across the ford and met in the middle of the river. All day long they hacked and struck at one another until each was bleeding from a score of wounds and the river ran red with their blood. At last, towards evening, Ferdia drove his sword into Cuchulain's body right to the hilt. Cuchulain staggered backwards and called to Laegh for Gae Bolg, and Ferdia knew it was the end. He held his battered shield before him, but Cuchulain hurled the terrible weapon and it passed through Ferdia's breastplate and right through his body.

'The battle is over, Cuchulain,' said Ferdia as he sank slowly to his knees in the reddened water.

Cuchulain flung down his arms and sprang to his side, forgetting the pain of his great wounds in the greater pain of his loss. Gently he picked him up and carried him to the northern bank of the river, so that Ferdia might die in Ulster, and not among Cuchulain's enemies.

'It is not as it should have been, that I have died at your hands, Little Hound,' whispered Ferdia. Then, while Cuchulain held him close in his arms, he died.

'I should have died too, with my Ferdia,' said Cuchulain, and, weeping, he made a lament for his friend.

> It was all a sport and a game,
> Until Ferdia came
> Against me.
>
> O valiant Ferdia, dearest friend,
> I shall to the very end
> Remember.
>
> A mountain was he yesterday,
> My Ferdia who is today
> A shadow.

After the death of Ferdia, Cuchulain fought no more against Maeve's champions, and Laegh carried him away from the river's bank to the safety of his house at Dun Dalgan.

When Sualtach, his foster-father, heard how he lay wounded and mourning, he came to him. But Cuchulain said, 'It is Ulster that has need of you, not I. Go, I beg you, rouse Conor and the Red Branch warriors, for I can fight no longer.'

Sualtach mounted the Grey of Battle and set off at once for Emain Macha. He rode into the hall where Conor and all his men lay sleeping and cried out, 'Our men are being slain, our women led away and our cattle driven off. Rise up and save Ulster.'

But no one heard him, save only Caffa the druid, who muttered in his sleep, 'You disturb the king's rest. Begone.'

In despair, Sualtach turned the Grey's head, meaning to ride back to Cuchulain, but he pulled on the reins too sharply, and the Grey of Battle reared. Sualtach, trying not to be thrown, leant forward too far and struck his neck on the sharp edge of his shield, so that his head was severed from his body and fell to the floor of the hall from where it went on crying out, 'Rise up, men of Ulster, and save your land,' until at last Conor heard it and opened his eyes and said sleepily, 'That head makes too much noise. Let someone put it on a pillar, out of the way.'

But Sualtach's head shouted more loudly than ever, and because it was almost time for the spell to pass from them, one by one the warriors of the Red Branch began to wake; and as they woke, they heard the words of the head and roused Conor, who sprang to his feet, calling for his arms. 'Unless the sky with all its stars falls down upon us, unless the seas rise over the land, or the earth gives way beneath us, I will restore every woman to her home and every cow to its byre,' he swore. And summoning all his men to Emain Macha, he led them southwards against Maeve.

Queen Maeve was standing on a hill looking towards Ulster. 'What is that mist that rolls over the plain?' she asked.

'It is the breath of the men and the horses in the army of King Conor,' answered Fergus Mac Roy.

'And what is that light like stars shining through the mist?'

'That is the eyes of the men of Ulster glinting with their anger,' said Fergus.

'What is that noise as of thunder that I can hear?'

'That is the hooves of the horses and the wheels of the chariots of the men of Ulster as they come out to battle.'

'And that flock of birds,' said Maeve, 'coming towards us. What is that, Fergus?'

'Those are no birds. Those are the sods of earth flung up by the hooves of the horses, so swiftly they come against us.' And Fergus Mac Roy smiled to himself, for he was a man of Ulster, for all he was fighting for Queen Maeve.

But she raised her proud head yet higher. 'Let them come. We are ready for them,' she said.

It was a terrible battle that they fought, the two great armies; and first one side and then the other seemed to be the stronger. Cuchulain took no part in it at first – though he would willingly have stood beside his comrades – for Laegh had bound him to his bed so that he should not go out to fight before his wounds were healed. But in the battle Fergus Mac Roy came face to face with Conor, whom he hated for the wrong which he had done to him and for his treachery to the sons of Usna. They fought together grimly, and three times Fergus struck with his sword upon Conor's shield. Now, the peculiarity of Conor Mac Nessa's shield was this, that when its owner was in danger, it would cry out for help. Lying on his bed in Dun Dalgan, Cuchulain heard Conor's shield cry and he struggled so hard that he burst his bonds; and with his wounds all bleeding afresh, he went into battle to save his king.

He reached the place where Conor fought with Fergus, and

even as Fergus raised his sword to strike down Conor, Cuchulain stood between them and cried out, 'Remember your promise to me, that day we met at the ford, Fergus. I fled from you that day. Flee you now from me and keep your word.'

Fergus kept his word and fled, and with him fled all his men; and seeing him, as they believed, defeated, all Maeve's allies fled after him, until only Maeve and Ailell and the finest of the warriors of Connaught still stood against the men of Ulster. But Maeve fought on until word was brought to her that the Brown Bull of Cooley was safely across the Shannon and well into her own land, then she, too, turned and fled; and, as the druid had foreseen, she returned safely home. And so ended the Cattle Raid of Cooley.

But although Maeve had won her bull, she had no profit of it, for the moment the Brown Bull of Cooley and the White-horned Bull of Connaught had sight of one another, they fought; and the Brown Bull gored and killed Ailell's White-horned Bull, and bellowing with triumph, raged about the country, making for his home in Ulster, until his heart burst and he fell dead.

For seven years there was peace between Ulster and Connaught; but Maeve could not forgive Cuchulain her defeat, for she would have had an easy victory had he not held her army back all through the winter months, alone; and she determined to kill him, no matter by what means.

She gathered together all who hated or envied Cuchulain, and ordered them northwards. Then she sent against him evil sorcerers, who put spells on him so that he thought the enemies of Ulster were ravaging the land; and in spite of all that his friends could do to persuade him the danger was all of his imagining, he ordered Laegh to make ready his chariot, that he might go out to fight. But when Laegh came to yoke the Grey of Battle to the chariot, the horse resisted, and was only subdued and bridled with difficulty, and then stood dejectedly, weeping tears of blood.

Cuchulain's mother, Dectera, handed him a cup of wine before he left her, but as he raised it to his lips, it turned to blood. And as he mounted his chariot, his weapons fell crashing to the ground.

'I shall not return from this battle,' said Cuchulain.

As Laegh drove southwards they crossed a stream, and at the ford was a maiden washing a bloodstained tunic. As they passed, she held it up and Cuchulain saw that it was his.

'It is the Washer of the Ford,' said Laegh, pale-faced. 'She washes the garments of those who are to die in battle. Let us turn back, Cuchulain.'

'We cannot turn back while Ulster is in danger,' said Cuchulain.

A little farther on they came upon three old hags cooking collops of hound's flesh over a fire. The women called out to Cuchulain, bidding him share their meal. He refused, for it was forbidden him to eat the flesh of the animal which was his namesake. But they upbraided him, saying, 'You are ready enough to eat with the rich and the mighty, yet you scorn the hospitality of the poor.' So he stopped and ate with them before going on his way.

When he came to where his enemies waited for him, on the edge of a lake, once more he was one against a whole army. He had three spears with him and of each of these spears it had been said that it would kill a king. He flung one spear amongst his enemies, and they flung it back against him, missing him but killing Laegh – who was the king of charioteers. He flung the second spear, and they hurled it back at him, striking the Grey of Battle – a king among horses. The Black of the Glen reared and struggled and broke free from the chariot, galloping wildly away. Cuchulain threw his third spear, and his enemies took it up and flung it back, and Cuchulain – the king of warriors – fell, wounded to death.

Maeve's men stood around him, at a safe distance, watching him as he struggled to raise himself. 'I am thirsty,' he said. 'Let me drink from the lake.' He rose to his feet and staggered to the lakeside, knelt down and drank and washed the blood from his wound. Then, seeing a pillar stone at the edge of the water, he went slowly to it, and standing with his back against it, he tied himself to it with his girdle, so that he might die upon his feet and facing his enemies, with his arm still upraised and holding his sword. His face grew pale and the light went out of it, and after a while a crow came to perch upon his shoulder.

Then, when they were sure that he was dead, his enemies came closer, and one man there cut off his head to take to Maeve; but even as he did so, the sword fell from Cuchulain's grasp and struck off the man's hand.

And so ended Cuchulain, the Hound of Ulster, the greatest of all Irish heroes.

Dermot and Grania

Finn and the Fianna, according to popular tradition, lived in the third century A.D., three hundred years later than Cuchulain and the heroes of the Red Branch are said to have fought and loved in Ulster; and the stories told of them are certainly not so ancient, nor so close to the divine myths of the Celts as the tales told of Cuchulain and Conor and their companions. Yet, for all that, the roots of these stories are old enough, and in them the heroes associate as familiarly with the gods as ever did Conor and the warriors of the earlier cycle of legends. In the following story, the hero, Dermot O'Dyna, is foster-child to the god of love.

This tale shows Finn Mac Cool as an older man than in the adventures retold in the Scottish section; and though in it the reader's sympathy is bound to be with Dermot, Finn is far from being the villain of the story. And if he always seems to know a lot, it must be remembered that he had tasted the Salmon of Knowledge.

Oisin, whose name means 'fawn', was Finn's son by Sadb, who was changed into a deer and stolen away from Finn by a dark enchanter – one of the gods.

THERE came a day when Manissa, wife of Finn Mac Cool, the great warrior and chief leader of the Fianna, died, and Finn, no longer young, was sad and lonely without a wife to cheer and comfort him. 'You should take another wife,' said Oisin, his son.

'There is Grania, daughter of King Cormac. She is said to be the loveliest maid in all Ireland, and she is yet unwed,' said Dering O'Baskin, one of the leaders of the Fianna. 'Why do you not take her for your wife, lord?'

So Finn sent Oisin and Dering to Tara, to ask for Grania's hand. Now, Grania, beautiful above all women and daughter of the High King of Ireland, was proud and had refused many suitors; but her father received Oisin and Dering kindly, and asked them their errand.

'We have come to seek the hand of Grania for Finn Mac Cool,' said Oisin.

'My daughter has refused all the kings in Ireland,' said Cormac. 'If she refuses Finn, it will be no fault of mine. But let you both come with me now, to hear her answer from her own lips, so that I shall have no blame of it.'

They went to the women's hall and Cormac said to Grania, 'Here are two warriors of the Fianna, come to ask you in marriage for Finn Mac Cool.'

Grania gave one haughty glance at them and turned away, answering carelessly, 'If he is a worthy son-in-law for you, my father, why should he not be a fitting husband for me?'

Oisin and Dering, satisfied with this answer, returned to Finn bearing a message from Cormac that Finn should come in fourteen days to fetch his bride. Accordingly, when the fourteen days were passed, Finn and all the leaders of the Fianna set out for Tara, where they found a great feast prepared for them.

While the feasting was at its height, Grania spoke with Dara of the Poems, who sat near her, and she asked him, 'Tell me, Dara, why has my father ordered a feast, and why has Finn come to Tara with all his warriors?'

Dara, surprised and disturbed, sought to evade the question

by saying, 'Truly, if you do not know, how should I know?'

But Grania demanded an answer, and fearing lest she should grow angry, Dara said, 'Do you not know that Finn has come to marry you?'

Grania was silent for a while, then she said, 'It would not have been strange had Finn asked me as a wife for his son Oisin, or even for his grandson, Oscar. But it is strange that he should seek me for himself, for he is older than my father.'

Then Grania looked about her, at all the Fianna sitting at the feast, and there was one amongst them whom she noticed more than the others. As though idly, and without a purpose, she turned again to Dara. 'Of all Finn's warriors, the only two I know by name are Oisin and Dering O'Baskin. Tell me, Dara, who is the fierce old warrior who sits on Oisin's right?'

'That is Gaul Mac Morna, the terrible in battle.'

'And the red-haired youth to the right of Gaul?'

'That is Oscar, the son of Oisin,' said Dara.

'And beside Oscar, that slim, lithe warrior?'

'That is Keelta Mac Ronan, the swift runner, fleetest of all the Fianna.'

'And beside Keelta,' said Grania, as though she cared nothing for the answer, 'who is that handsome warrior with the grey eyes and the auburn hair?'

'That,' replied Dara, 'is Dermot O'Dyna of the bright face, nephew of Finn and foster-child of Angus of the Birds himself. Dermot is a favourite with all maidens, and loved by all the Fianna for his courage and his worth.'

Having learnt what she wished, Grania asked no more, but sat awhile in silence and thought. Then she called to her one of her serving-women and whispered, 'Bring me my golden drinking-cup that is set with gems.' When it had been brought to her, Grania filled it with wine that would send the drinker into a deep sleep, and said, 'Take it now to Finn Mac Cool, and bid him drink from it.'

Finn drank a long draught from the cup and then handed it to King Cormac; he also drank, and after him, the queen. Then Grania sent the cup to all those whom she wished to drink from it, and by the time the cup was empty, all those who had drunk were fast asleep.

Then Grania rose and went down the hall to Dermot and sat beside him. 'Will you have my love, Dermot O'Dyna, and take me from this house with you?'

'You are Finn's bride,' said Dermot, appalled, 'and I am Finn's warrior. I will not take Finn's bride from him.'

'Finn is old and I do not love him. But you are young, Dermot, and you I love. Take me away from Tara to-night.'

'I will not, for Finn is my lord and I am true to him.'

'Then I will put you under bonds to do as I ask, and you cannot refuse,' declared Grania.

'Those are evil bonds and only evil can come of them,' said Dermot.

Grania rose and held out her hand to him. 'Come, Dermot.'

Greatly troubled, Dermot said to Oisin, 'Tell me, what shall I do?'

'You are not to blame that Grania has put bonds on you,' said Oisin. 'My counsel is that you do as she demands, but beware of my father's wrath.'

'My dear friend Oscar,' said Dermot, 'tell me, what should I do?'

'A warrior cannot break bonds that have been put on him,' said young Oscar. 'Go with Grania, Dermot.'

'And what is your counsel, Keelta?'

'My counsel is to follow Grania, Dermot.'

'And yours, Dering?'

'Nothing but ill, and your death, can come of it, Dermot

my friend,' said Dering. 'But go you with Grania, for no warrior may break his bonds.'

And Dermot looked about him at all his friends and asked, 'Is this the counsel of you all?'

And as one man the Fianna answered, 'It is.'

Sadly Dermot bade them farewell and went with Grania, knowing well that Finn would pursue them throughout all Ireland until he had avenged the wrong. Right across Ireland they wandered until they reached the Wood of the Two Tents, in Galway, and there in the wood Dermot built a little hut for Grania, where they stayed to rest themselves.

When Finn awoke and found Dermot and Grania gone, a great anger and jealousy seized him and he called for his trackers, the Clan Navin, and set them to follow the tracks of the fugitives. Finn and the Fianna went after the Clan Navin; and when they had been led into Galway, Finn said, 'We shall find them in the Wood of the Two Tents, I have no doubt.'

Oisin, Oscar, Keelta and Dering were grieved when they heard Finn speak these words, for they loved Dermot and did not wish Finn to catch him. They went apart together and wondered how they might help their friend.

Then Oisin said to his son, 'Go, Oscar, send Bran into the Wood of the Two Tents with a warning to Dermot, for Bran loves Dermot almost as well as he loves his master.'

So, with no word to Finn, Oscar fetched Bran, Finn's hound, and whispered to him what he should do: and the hound understood. Then Bran ran swiftly off, following the tracks of Dermot and Grania, right into the Wood of the Two Tents. In the very middle of the wood he found Dermot and Grania asleep in their hut, and he woke Dermot, thrusting his muzzle against Dermot's cheek.

Dermot sat up and cried out, 'See, Grania, here is Bran, Finn's hound. Finn himself cannot be far off.'

'Let us fly then,' said Grania, trembling.

'However far we fly,' said Dermot, 'we cannot escape Finn. And if he is to catch us, it is as well now as at any other time. I shall not leave this place.' And he built a fence all about the hut, having seven narrow gateways in it, facing seven different ways.

Dermot's friends were still afraid for him, and Oisin said, 'What if Bran should not have found Dermot? Keelta, fetch Fergor, your messenger.' And when Keelta had sent for him, Oisin bade Fergor give three shouts. Now, Fergor had a voice so loud that it could be heard across three cantreds, and when he gave his shouts, Dermot heard him in the wood and said to Grania, 'That is the shout of Fergor, Keelta's messenger. That is a warning from my friends that Finn is here.'

'Let us fly,' said Grania again.

'I shall not leave this place, and no one shall come in,' said Dermot. And he took up his weapons and waited.

Sending the Clan Navin ahead of him and following with the Fianna, Finn came into the Wood of the Two Tents, and in the middle of the wood he came upon a tall fence. One of the trackers climbed a tree and looked over the fence, saw Dermot and Grania and, coming down, told Finn.

'Before he leaves this wood,' said Finn, 'Dermot shall pay in full for the wrong he has done me.'

'Were you not blinded by jealousy,' said Oisin, 'you would not believe Dermot to be so foolish as to wait here for you to come to him, with no more between him and you than a wooden fence.'

Then Finn grew even more angry than he was, and he exclaimed, 'Your friendship will bring little profit to Dermot, Oisin. Well do I know how you sent Bran to him and made Fergor shout three times to warn him. But he shall not escape me.'

'It is folly,' said Oscar desperately. 'Indeed, Dermot is not here.'

'I shall soon show you which of us is right,' said Finn. And he called out in a loud voice, 'Dermot, tell me, which of us speaks truly, Oscar or I?'

And from inside the fence Dermot answered, 'It is you who speak truly, lord. I am here with Grania. But no one shall come in to us.'

Then Finn divided up his men so that they stood before each of the seven narrow gateways, with orders to take Dermot and bind him if he tried to escape. He himself went a little way off to a small hill from where he could see over the fence, and he saw how Grania trembled and was afraid, and how Dermot put his arm about her and kissed her, bidding her have courage. And at the sight Finn's anger and jealousy were increased a hundredfold. 'Now, by the gods, Dermot shall not escape,' he swore. He came down from the hill and set himself at one of the seven gates, his drawn sword in his hand.

When Angus of the Birds, god of love, the foster-father of Dermot, saw his plight, he travelled swiftly on the wind until he came to the hut within the fence in the midst of the Wood of the Two Tents. Unseen of any save Dermot and Grania, he stretched out his cloak and said, 'Come you now under my cloak, and we shall all three pass out of here unknown to Finn.'

But Dermot would not go with him. 'I am a warrior,' he said. 'Shall I fly like a coward from danger? Yet take Grania with you, and I shall follow if I can.' So Angus of the Birds went swiftly away with Grania to a wood in that place which is now called Limerick.

Then Dermot put on his brazen breastplate and helmet and took up two tall spears, and he went to the first of the narrow gateways in the fence. 'Who is outside?' he asked.

'No one but Oisin and Oscar. Come out at this gate, Dermot, and go free.'

'I will not,' said Dermot, 'for you are my good friends and I would not bring trouble upon you.' He passed on to the second gateway. 'Who is here?' he asked.

'Keelta Mac Ronan and the Clan Ronan. Come out at this gate and we will fight to the death for you, Dermot.'

'I will not,' said Dermot, 'for I would not bring Finn's anger on you.' And he passed to the third gateway. 'Who is here?'

'Conan of the Grey Rushes and the Clan Morna. Come out at this gate and no one will harm you, Dermot.'

'I will not, for I know that Finn would rather see you all dead, than that I should escape him.' And Dermot passed on to the fourth gateway. 'Who is here?'

'An old friend of yours, Dermot. Cuan of Munster and his men. Come out through this gate, for we are ready to give our lives for you.'

'I will not,' said Dermot. 'I would not have you at enmity with Finn.' And he passed on to the fifth gateway. 'Who is here?'

'Finn Mac Glore of the loud voice and his men. Come out at this gate, Dermot, for we are all well disposed towards you.'

'I will not, for you are a loyal friend, and your father was my friend also, and I would not earn you Finn's hatred.' And he passed on to the sixth gateway. 'Who is here?'

'No friends of yours, Dermot O'Dyna. Here is Clan Navin the trackers waiting for you. Come out at this gate, Dermot, and be a target for our spears and our swords.'

'Curs and cowards!' said Dermot. 'I will not. And not from any fear of you, but because I would not sully my spear with your blood.' And he passed on to the seventh gateway. 'Who is here?'

'Finn Mac Cool is here, Dermot, and if you come out

through this gate you will be hewn in little pieces, flesh and bones.'

'This is the gate that I have been seeking. I am coming out, Finn!' And Dermot took a run and a jump and rose up by means of his two spears and was over the heads of Finn and those waiting with him and away through the wood before ever they realized what he was about. So Dermot escaped, and hastening southwards he came to where Grania waited with Angus of the Birds.

Then Angus left them together; but he gave them this warning before he went, 'Finn will never leave his vengeance, so beware of him. Never go into a tree having only one trunk; never enter a cave that has no more than one opening; never land on an island that has but one harbour. Where you cook your food, do not eat it; where you eat, do not sleep; and where you sleep tonight, do not sleep there tomorrow.'

And so Dermot and Grania wandered on, following the counsel of Angus of the Birds. Many escapes they had from those whom Finn sent to pursue them, and they never spent more than a day in any one place, until they were weary beyond belief of never being at rest. And then they came at last to the Forest of Dooros, in Sligo. In this forest grew a magic rowan tree which was at that time guarded by a giant, Sharvan the Surly, with one red eye in the middle of his forehead.

'I have had enough of wandering, Dermot,' said Grania. 'Let us stay here in this place.'

'Finn will hardly follow us here,' said Dermot. And he made a bargain with the giant, that he would touch none of the berries from the tree, nor come near to it; and in return Sharvan gave him leave to build a hut for himself and Grania, and to hunt the beasts of the forest for food. And so they remained for a while, in peace. But Finn had not forgotten them.

There were at that time two men of the Clan Morna with

whom Finn had a feud, for the sake of their fathers' deeds against his father. These two men now wished to make peace with Finn, and they came to him and asked that they might be numbered among the Fianna. Finn said that he would agree to this if they would bring him one of two things, either a handful of berries from the magic rowan tree of Dooros, or the head of Dermot O'Dyna.

'You will not come by either easily,' said Oisin, who was standing near while his father spoke.

'Nevertheless, we will attempt one or the other,' said the two men, and they set off for the Forest of Dooros to try their luck with the magic berries, for they had no idea where Dermot might be found. When they came to the edge of the forest, they saw the hut where Dermot was living with Grania, but they did not know who he was. Dermot took up his weapons and went to meet them. 'Who are you, strangers?' he asked.

They told him their names, and said that Finn Mac Cool had a feud with them which he would end only if they brought him the head of Dermot O'Dyna or a handful of berries from the magic rowan tree. 'And so,' they said, 'we are here to pick the berries from the tree.'

'Why should Finn want the berries?' asked Dermot.

The men smiled. 'Who would not want them? If all that we have heard concerning them is true, they are most wonderful, for if anyone who is sick should eat of them, he will be well in an instant. The old who eat of them will become young again, and but one berry will fill a man with joy and courage.'

'Truly,' exclaimed Grania, 'those are wondrous berries. I would I had some of them.'

Dermot laughed when he heard the quest of the men of Clan Morna. 'Indeed, my friends, the luck is with you, for you came on one quest and find the other waiting for you. I am Dermot O'Dyna. Which will you take first, the berries or my head? I warn you, you will not win either easily.'

'We will take your head,' they said.

So they undertook to fight Dermot without weapons, and it was agreed that if one of them could overcome him in wrestling, he might cut off his head and take it to Finn. They wrestled, but Dermot was more than a match for both of them, and one after the other he threw them and bound them fast, while Grania looked on. When it was done she came to him and said, 'Dermot, fetch me some of those berries of which they spoke, for I have a great desire to taste them.'

'I made a bargain with the giant,' said Dermot. 'Would you have me break it?'

'I shall die if I do not eat of those berries,' she said.

'Release us, and we will pick the berries for her,' said the two men of Clan Morna.

'No, I shall pick them myself,' said Dermot, 'though little good will come of it.' But he freed the two men, that they might go with him to watch what befell.

When they came to the rowan tree, Sharvan was asleep and Dermot woke him, saying, 'Give me some berries from your tree, for Grania, daughter of the High King of Ireland, wishes to eat of them.'

'She shall not,' said the giant, and he jumped up swinging his great club. But Dermot leapt aside, and flinging himself at the giant, brought him to the ground. Then he snatched the giant's own club from him and cracked open his head with it. The men of Clan Morna buried Sharvan in the forest while Dermot picked berries from the tree for Grania and for the two men, bidding them take the berries to Finn. When they had gone on their way, Dermot and Grania climbed the rowan tree to where the giant had built a house for himself on a platform among the branches, and there they lived.

The men of Clan Morna returned to Finn and gave him

the berries, saying, 'The giant Sharvan is dead and here are the berries you wished. Now accept us into the Fianna, as you promised.'

But Finn took the berries and smelled them and he said, 'It was Dermot O'Dyna who picked these berries, for I can smell the touch of his hand on them. And no doubt it was Dermot, not you, who slew the giant. I shall go myself to the Forest of Dooros and see if he is there, for I have a score to settle with him.' And he called together the Fianna and set out.

When they came to the rowan tree they found no one there to guard it, and neither Dermot nor Grania was in sight, for they were hidden high up in the branches of the tree. And because it was noon and the sun was hot, Finn said, 'Let us sit here and rest, for Dermot is near by.' And he sat down below the tree.

'Truly, your wits are dimmed by jealousy,' said Oisin. 'How should Dermot be near by, when he knows you are after his head?'

Finn called for his chessmen and bade Oisin play with him. Because Finn was so skilled at chess, Oscar and Dering sat beside Oisin and gave him their help, and Finn played against the three of them. And well and cunningly he played, until at last there was only the one move that Oisin could make: and that one move would have won him the game, but that he did not know what move it was.

'One move and you have won, Oisin,' laughed Finn. 'I challenge you and your friends to make it.'

As they looked at the board, puzzled, Dermot, who had been watching the game through the branches, whispered to himself, 'It is hard that you should lose the game, and I not by to help you.'

'Who cares whether Oisin lose a game of chess or not?' said Grania. 'The tree is surrounded by all the Fianna, and you are likely to lose your head.'

But Dermot paid no heed to her. He plucked a berry and dropped it down on to that chessman which Oisin should move, and Oisin moved it and won the game.

Finn called for another game, and again it happened as before. Oisin had but one move left to make and again Dermot dropped a berry on to the piece which was to be moved, and Oisin won the game. Then Finn called for a third game, and yet again it was the same Dermot won for Oisin.

Finn said drily, 'Small wonder that you should win three games from me, Oisin, since you have not only the help of Oscar and Dering, but also Dermot's skill to aid you.'

'Your mind is bemused by jealousy, if you believe Dermot is in that tree, waiting for you to kill him,' said Oscar quickly.

Finn glanced up into the branches of the tree. 'Which of us speaks truly, Dermot, Oscar or I?' he asked.

'As always, lord, you are right,' said Dermot. 'Grania and I are here, up in the rowan tree.' And he thrust aside the branches that they could see him. At this Grania began to weep, and Dermot put his arms about her and kissed her to comfort her, so that Finn grew very angry and said, 'You shall pay for those kisses with your head, Dermot.' And he called for any of his men who would climb the tree and fetch down Dermot or his head.

Garva of Slieve Cua stepped forward saying, 'It was Dermot's father who slew my father. I will now avenge his death,' and he climbed up the tree. But Dermot flung him down to the ground again, and, as he fell, Angus of the Birds, coming swiftly, put the appearance of Dermot on him, so that Garva's friends killed him as he reached the ground. But the moment he was dead, Angus gave him back his own appearance, so that they saw it was Garva they had killed.

Another man then climbed the tree, and it was the same with him; and so it was until nine men had been slain, thanks to the aid of Angus of the Birds, and Finn was growing more angry and more bitter every moment.

Then Angus said that he would bear Grania away from danger, and Dermot was glad. 'Take her,' he said, 'and if I live, I will follow you.' Angus of the Birds wrapped his cloak about Grania and bore her away, unseen by any, leaving Dermot alone in the tree. Dermot called down to Finn, 'I see that you are determined on my death. I am coming down now, and I shall kill as many of your men as I may, before I die myself. I am not afraid to die, Finn, which is as well, since there can be no escape for me. In days past I made myself too many enemies throughout all Ireland, fighting your battles for you. There is no man to help me now. Those few who would, dare not for fear of you.'

'It is true what he says,' begged Oscar. 'Forgive him, Finn. Let him have peace now, for he has suffered enough.'

'He will have no peace until I have his head,' said Finn.

'Then,' said Oscar, 'I pledge my word that the sky will sooner fall on me, or the earth open to swallow me up, than that I will let any man harm Dermot.' He looked up into the tree. 'Come down, Dermot, for here stands one man who does not fear to help you and none shall touch you while I live to guard you.'

Hidden by the leaves of the rowan tree, Dermot walked to the end of one of the long branches and then he leapt lightly outwards and downwards, and came to the ground well beyond the circle of men who stood around the tree. Young Oscar ran to join him, and together they fled from the Forest of Dooros and made their way to the Boyne, where they found Angus waiting for them with Grania.

After a time Angus of the Birds went to Finn and bade him make peace with Dermot, and at the bidding of the god, Finn did so, though in his heart he could not forgive him. Dermot took back his father's lands and he and Grania lived for sev-

eral years in peace, far from Finn and the Fianna; until there came a day when Grania, whose demands had ever cost Dermot dear, said, 'It is unfitting that we should live in this manner, far from good company, never visited by the High King, my father, nor by Finn Mac Cool. Let us give a feast for them and bid them come here to our house.'

'There is peace between Finn and myself, yet we are enemies for all that. Let things remain as they are, Grania,' said Dermot.

But she would not, and in the end he did as she urged him and made a great feast lasting many days for Finn and the Fianna and King Cormac and his lords. By day Dermot and his guests hunted together and all evening they ate and drank and made merry.

But one morning as they were hunting, Dermot faced a huge boar alone. He killed it, yet it had gored him, and when Finn and the Fianna reached him, they found him dying on the ground. The Fianna cried out with distress, but Finn stood looking down on Dermot and he said, 'I am not sorry to see you thus, Dermot.'

'Surely those words come only from your lips and not from your heart, Finn,' said Dermot. 'You know that you can save me, if you will.'

'How can I save you?' asked Finn.

'Well you know, Finn, that the gift of saving life was given to you, many years ago, and that any man who drinks water from the closed palms of your two hands shall be healed of all wounds or sickness, no matter if he be dying.'

'That is true,' said Finn. 'But why should I save your life? Surely of all men, you deserve it least from me.'

'I have served you well in the past, lord.'

'You stole Grania from me.'

'One day you may need my help again,' whispered Dermot weakly.

Oscar wept. 'No more than a drink from your hands would save him. Give him water, Finn.'

'There is no spring nearby,' said Finn.

'You lie,' said Dermot. 'There is a spring beneath that bush, no more than nine paces from here.'

Finn turned away and went to the spring and filled his cupped hands with water, and he came slowly back to Dermot. But when he was still three or four paces off, he remembered Grania, and he opened his hands and the water trickled out. 'I cannot carry water so far in my hands,' he said.

'That is not true, Finn,' said Dermot. 'Hurry, for I am almost dead.'

Finn went again to the spring, but as he was returning with the water, he thought once more of Grania. He let the water trickle through his fingers, and Dermot groaned.

Oscar cried out in anguish, 'If you do not bring the water, I swear that only one of us – you or I – will leave this place alive, Finn.'

Then Finn fetched water a third time, and hastened, for he loved his grandson above all other men; but before he could hold the water to Dermot's lips, Dermot's head had fallen back upon the grass, and he was dead.

All the Fianna raised a cry of sorrow for Dermot, and Oscar and Oisin and Dering wept for him. After a time Finn said, 'Let us go now, for Angus of the Birds may be wrathful and blame us for Dermot's death.' He took up the leash of Dermot's boarhound, and led the hound away, and the Fianna followed silently. But Oisin and Oscar and Dering, still weeping, stayed long enough to cover Dermot with their cloaks, before they, too, went after Finn.

*

In a Scottish version of this story, Finn causes Dermot's death by ordering him to measure the skin of the boar which he has killed, by pacing the length out with his bare feet. Dermot does so and is pricked by one of the boar's poisonous bristles, just as Finn had hoped.

It is in remembrance of Dermot's boar that the Clan Campbell, which claims descent from him, took a boar as its emblem.

A Note on the Pronunciation

I HAVE made no attempt to be consistent in the spelling of the Gaelic names in this book. In nearly every case I have chosen that particular anglicized form which I considered, for one reason or another, to be the most suitable; and in one or two instances, where I felt the anglicizations to be unhelpful, I have kept to a Gaelic form.

The pronunciation of Gaelic – which is far from easy – varies from district to district, both in Ireland and in the Scottish Highlands. All the pronunciations given in the following list are only approximate, but they should be sufficiently close for general purposes.

The Welsh vowel sounds given are rather closer to those of South Wales than to those heard in the north of the country.

All those names occurring in the stories, which do not appear in the list below, may be pronounced as if English.

Key to the Pronunciation

aw as in *lawn*

ay as in *day*

ah as the sound of *a* in *father*

air as in *pair*

ă as in *comma* rather than as in *hat*

ee as in *see*

ĕ as in *red*

er as in *pert*

ī as in *time*

ĭ as in *ship*

ō as in *robe*

ŏ as in *dog*

oo as in *gloom*

ŏŏ as in *good*

ow as in *now*

TH as in *that*

th as in *thing*

g as in *get*

H is used to indicate the sound of *ch* as in the Scottish *loch* or the German *ich*

Stressed syllables are shown by a stress mark (′) placed after the syllable which is stressed.

Ailell (āl′yĕl)

Ainnli (ĕn′lĭ)

Bedivere (bĕd′ĭ-vair)

Bedwyr (bĕd′weer)

Borrach (bŏr′rahH)

Bran, Finn's hound (brăn)

Bran, son of Llyr (brahn)

Branwen (brăn′wĕn)

Buinni the Red (boō′ĭn-nĭ)

Caradawc (kă-ră′dowk)

Ceridwen (kĕ-rĭd′wĕn)

Conor Mac Nessa (kŏn′awr măk nĕs′să)

Cuan (kōō′ăn)

Cuchulain (kōō-Hōōl′ĭn)

Culann (kōōl′ăn)

Dara (dah′ră)

Dectera (dĕk′tĕ-ră)

Deirdre (dee′er-drĭ)

Dyved (dĭv′ĕd)

Emain Macha (ĕv′ăn mah′Hă)

Evnissyen (ĕv-nĭss′yĕn)

Felim (fee′lĭm)

Ferdia (ferd′yă)

Fianna (fee′ăn-nă)

Gae Bolg (gay bŏl′ĕg)

Gawaine (gah′wayn)

geasa (gĕs′ă)

geis (gaysh)

Gillie Mairtean (gĭl′lĭ mahr′tĕn)

Grania (grahn′yă)

Griflet (gree-flay′)

Guenever (gwĕn′ĕv-er)

Gwalchmei (gwahlH′mĭ)

Gwawl (gwowl)

Gwent Is Coed (gwĕnt ĭss coyd)

Gwern (gwairn)

Gwion (gwee′ŏn)

Gwyddno (gwĭTH′nō)

Heinin (hĭ′nĭn)

Heveydd Hen (hĕv′ĭTH hayn)

Ian Direach (ee′ăn dee′rahH)

Igraine (ee-grayn′)

Illan the Fair (ĭl′lăn)

Kei (kĭ)

Laegh (layH)

Lavarcham (lay′vahr-Hăm)

Leodegrance (lay′ō-dĕ-grahns′)

Lleu Llaw Gyffes (hlĭ hlow gĭf′fĕss)

Llyr (hleer)

Lochlann (lŏH′lăn)

Lugh (lōoH)

Maelgwn Gwynedd (mĭl'gōōn gwĭn'ĕTH)

Maeve (mayv)

Maini (mă'nĭ)

Manannan Mac Lir (măn'ăn-ăn măk leer)

Manawyddan (măn-ă-wĭTH'ăn)

Matholwch (măth-ŏl'ōōH)

Medb (mayv)

Medrawt (mĕd'rowt)

Naoise (nee'shĭ)

Nissyen (nĭss'yĕn)

Oisin (ŏsh'een)

Pellinore (pĕl'lĭn-or)

Pryderi (prĭ-day'rĭ)

Pwyll (pwĭl)

Rhiannon (ree-ăn'nŏn)

Rhun (reen)

Sadb (sahv)

Scatha (skah'hă)

sidhe (shee)

Skolaun (skō'lawn)

Sualtach (sōōl'tahH)

Taliesin (tă-lĭ-ay'sĭn)

Teirnyon (tīr'nyŏn)

Usna (ōōsh'nă)

Uther (y'ōōther)

Vortigern (vawr'tĭ-gern)

THE YOUNG PRETENDERS

Romantic Jacobite, or poacher, vagabond, or thief? What kind of man was the handsome, dishevelled fugitive whom Francis and Annabel Rimpole had discovered in their father's park in the North Riding?

So began a long period of anxious and dangerous deception, concealing the fugitive in the dower house and smuggling food to him by night, till they could help him get farther away. And always the wavering and anxious doubts would slip into their minds – was their friend really all he seemed, and were his tales of battles and adventure true?

This exciting story is also a remarkable character study of the Rimpoles and their mysterious protégé, with many side-lights on eighteenth-century life and attitudes thrown in.

For readers of 10 and over.

A BOOK OF HEROES

edited by William Mayne

Here are all sorts of heroes and all kinds of heroism, gathered together from all the corners of the globe. Some of the heroes are familiar. There is Orlando, whose exploits at the Battle of Roncesvalles were sung at the Battle of Hastings in 1066. There is a fleet of sea heroes – Sir Francis Drake, Sir Richard Grenville, John Paul Jones. But there are also many less known stories, like the one about Kagssagssuk, the homeless Eskimo boy who became so strong he could wring a bear's neck with his bare hands. Or the one about Volund the crippled smith tricking wicked King Nidud.

For readers of 8 to 12.

THE HIGH DEEDS OF FINN MAC COOL

Rosemary Sutcliff

In the proud and far back days, when Ireland was called Erin, there was a band of heroic warriors called the Fianna. Theirs was the task of guarding the shores of their country and controlling the blood feuds of the five kingdoms into which Erin was divided, and their most glorious time was when their leader was a hero named Finn Mac Cool.

VIKING'S DAWN
THE ROAD TO MIKLAGARD
VIKING'S SUNSET

Henry Treece

Jointly described as A Viking Saga, the three books were designed by Henry Treece to be read as a complete epic. They follow the life cycle of Harald Sigurdson from the time when, as a young boy, he joins the crew of a Viking ship and comes marauding to our shores in search of treasure, until his last 'sunset' voyage when, pursuing marauders who have broken the peace of his own country, the Viking longboat loses course and is obliged to make an epic voyage which takes them finally to North America.

'Vikings,' says a character in one of these marvellously exciting books, 'are tied to salt water as a prisoner is tied with chains. There's no understanding them, they are either madmen or heroes.'

Compulsive and worthwhile reading for anyone over nine.

DRAGON SLAYER: The Story of Beowulf

Rosemary Sutcliff

Lion-hearted Beowulf, the hero who had the strength of thirty men in his arms, sailed away over the whale road to rid the Danes of their deadly scourge, the prowling monster who struck terror into the bravest warriors of Denmark as they waited night after night in King Hrothgar's court. Great glory came to Beowulf before he died, the renown from his three great battles, with Grendel and his fearful mother, and with the dragon who guarded the brilliant treasure-hoard hidden away in the earth.

Rosemary Sutcliff's retelling of the Anglo-Saxon epic *Beowulf* grasps the splendour and mystery of the original poem. It is a story to feed the imagination powerfully, and fill the mind with a trembling awe.

LEGIONS OF THE EAGLE

Henry Treece

This is the story of a boy who lived at the time of the first real Roman invasion of Britain. It is also a story of battle and treachery, as might be expected where so many peoples were living together, each with its own kings and heroes and beliefs. But at the end you will see that the point the tale tries to make is that it doesn't matter what colour your hair is, or what language you speak. The important thing is – what sort of person are you?

For boys and girls between nine and twelve.

If you have enjoyed this book and would like to know about others which we publish, why not join the Puffin Club? You will receive the club magazine, *Puffin Post*, four times a year and a smart badge and membership book. You will also be able to enter all the competitions. For details of cost and an application form, send a stamped addressed envelope to:

The Puffin Club Dept A
Penguin Books Limited
Bath Road
Harmondsworth
Middlesex